Robert Michael Ballantyne

The Prairie Chief

A Tale

Robert Michael Ballantyne

The Prairie Chief
A Tale

ISBN/EAN: 9783744723985

Printed in Europe, USA, Canada, Australia, Japan

Cover: Foto ©Andreas Hilbeck / pixelio.de

More available books at **www.hansebooks.com**

THE PRAIRIE CHIEF

A TALE

BY R. M. BALLANTYNE,

AUTHOR OF "THE ROVER OF THE ANDES;" "THE WILD MAN OF THE WEST;" "THE RED
ERIC;" "FREAKS ON THE FELLS;" "THE YOUNG TRAWLER;" "DUSTY DIAMONDS;"
"THE BATTERY AND THE BOILER;" "THE GIANT OF THE NORTH;" "POST HASTE;
A TALE OF HER MAJESTY'S MAILS;" "IN THE TRACK OF THE TROOPS;"
"THE SETTLER AND THE SAVAGE;" "UNDER THE WAVES;" "RIVERS
OF ICE;" "BLACK IVORY;" "THE PIRATE CITY;" "THE NORSEMEN
IN THE WEST;" "THE IRON HORSE;" "THE FLOATING LIGHT;"
"ERLING THE BOLD;" "FIGHTING THE FLAMES;"
"SHIFTING WINDS;" "DEEP DOWN;" "THE
LIGHTHOUSE;" "GASCOYNE;" "THE LIFEBOAT;"
"THE GOLDEN DREAM;" "THE LONELY
ISLAND;" ETC. ETC.

With Illustrations.

LONDON:

JAMES NISBET & CO., 21 BERNERS STREET.

1886.

PREFACE.

IF the reader should be tempted, while perusing the extraordinary incidents of this Tale, to think the hero thereof too good, too wise, too absurd, too romantic—too anything, let it be borne in mind that there are exceptional characters among North American Indians, as among other savages and ourselves.

This fact will account for much.

R. M. B.

HARROW-ON-THE-HILL, 1886.

LIST OF ILLUSTRATIONS.

THE PRAIRIE CHIEF:

A TALE.

——◆——

CHAPTER I.

THE ALARM.

WHITEWING was a Red Indian of the North American prairies. Though not a chief of the highest standing, he was a very great man in the estimation of his tribe, for, besides being possessed of qualities which are highly esteemed among all savages—such as courage, strength, agility, and the like—he was a deep thinker, and held speculative views in regard to the Great Manitou (God), as well as the ordinary affairs of life, which perplexed even the oldest men of his tribe, and induced the younger men to look on him as a profound mystery.

Indeed the feelings of the latter towards Whitewing amounted almost to veneration, for while, on the one

A

hand, he was noted as one of the most fearless among the braves, and a daring assailant of that king of the northern wilderness the grizzly bear, he was on the other hand modest and retiring—never boasted of his prowess, disbelieved in the principle of revenge, which to most savages is not only a pleasure but a duty, and refused to decorate his sleeves or leggings with the scalp-locks of his enemies. Indeed he had been known to allow more than one enemy to escape from his hand in time of war when he might easily have killed him. Altogether, Whitewing was a monstrous puzzle to his fellows, and much beloved by many of them.

The only ornament which he allowed himself was the white wing of a ptarmigan. Hence his name. This. symbol of purity was bound to his forehead by a band of red cloth wrought with the quills of the porcupine. It had been made for him by a dark-eyed girl whose name was an Indian word signifying " light heart." But let it not be supposed that Lightheart's head was like her heart. On the contrary, she had a good sound brain, and, although much given to laughter, jest, and raillery among her female friends, would listen with unflagging patience and profound solemnity to her lover's soliloquies in reference to things past, present, and to come.

One of the peculiarities of Whitewing was that he did not treat women as mere slaves or inferior creatures.

His own mother, a wrinkled, brown old thing resembling a piece of singed shoe-leather, he loved with a tenderness not usual in North American Indians, some tribes of whom have a tendency to forsake their aged ones, and leave them to perish rather than be burdened with them. Whitewing also thought that his betrothed was fit to hold intellectual converse with him, in which idea he was not far wrong.

At the time we introduce him to the reader he was on a visit to the Indian camp of Lightheart's tribe in Clearvale, for the purpose of claiming his bride. His own tribe, of which the celebrated old warrior Bald Eagle was chief, dwelt in a valley at a considerable distance from the camp referred to.

There were two other visitors at the Indian camp at that time. One was a Wesleyan missionary who had penetrated to that remote region with a longing desire to carry the glad tidings of salvation in Jesus to the red men of the prairie. The other was a nondescript little white trapper, who may be aptly described as a mass of contradictions. He was small in stature, but amazingly strong; ugly, one-eyed, scarred in the face, and misshapen; yet wonderfully attractive, because of a sweet smile, a hearty manner, and a kindly disposition. With the courage of the lion, Little Tim, as he was styled, combined the agility of the monkey and the laziness of the sloth.

Strange to say, Tim and Whitewing were bosom friends, although they differed in opinion on most things.

"The white man speaks again about Manitou to-day," said the Indian, referring to the missionary's intention to preach, as he and Little Tim concluded their midday meal in the wigwam that had been allotted to them.

"It's little I cares for that," replied Tim curtly, as he lighted the pipe with which he always wound up every meal.

Of course both men spoke in the Indian language, but that being probably unknown to the reader, we will try to convey in English as nearly as possible the slightly poetical tone of the one and the rough Backwoods' style of the other.

"It seems strange to me," returned the Indian, "that my white brother thinks and cares so little about his Manitou. He thinks much of his gun, and his traps, and his skins, and his powder, and his friend, but cares not for Manitou, who gave him all these—all that he possesses."

"Look 'ee here, Whitewing," returned the trapper, in his matter-of-fact way, "there's nothing strange about it. I see you, and I see my gun and these other things, and can handle 'em; but I don't know nothin' about Manitou, and I don't *see* him, so what's the good o' thiukin' about him?"

Instead of answering, the red man looked silently and wistfully up into the blue sky, which could be seen through the raised curtain of the wigwam. Then, pointing to the landscape before them, he said in subdued but earnest tones—

"*I* see him in the clouds—in the sun, and moon, and stars; in the prairies and in the mountains; I hear him in the singing waters and in the winds that scatter the leaves, and I feel him *here.*"

Whitewing laid his hand on his breast, and looked in his friend's face.

"But," he continued sadly, "I do not understand him. He whispers so softly that though I hear I cannot comprehend. I wonder why this is so."

"Ay, that's just it, Whitewing," said the trapper. "We can't make it out nohow, an' so I just leaves all that sort o' thing to the parsons, and give my mind to the things that I understand."

"When Little Tim was a very small boy," said the Indian, after a few minutes' meditation, "did he understand how to trap the beaver and the martin, and how to point the rifle so as to carry death to the grizzly bear?"

"Of course not," returned the trapper; "seems to me that that's a foolish question."

"But," continued the Indian, "you came to know it at last?"

"I should just think I did," returned the trapper, a look of self-satisfied pride crossing his scarred visage as he thought of the celebrity as a hunter to which he had attained. "It took me a goodish while, of course, to circumvent it all, but in time I got to be—well, you know what, an' I'm not fond o' blowin' my own trumpet."

"Yes; you came to it at last," repeated Whitewing, "by giving your mind to things that at first you *did not understand.*"

"Come, come, my friend," said Little Tim, with a laugh; "I'm no match for you in argiment, but, as I said before, I don't understand Manitou, an' I don't see, or feel, or hear him, so it's of no use tryin'."

"What my friend knows not, another may tell him," said Whitewing. "The white man says he knows Manitou, and brings a message from him. Three times I have listened to his words. They seem the words of truth. I go again to-day to hear his message."

The Indian stood up as he spoke, and the trapper also rose.

"Well, well," he said, knocking the ashes out of his pipe, "I'll go too, though I'm afeared it won't be o' much use."

The sermon which the man of God preached that day to the Indians was neither long nor profound, but it was delivered with the intense earnestness of one who thoroughly believes every word he utters, and feels that life and death may be trembling in the balance with those who listen. It is not our purpose to give this sermon in detail, but merely to show its influence on Whitewing, and how it affected the stirring incidents which followed.

Already the good man had preached three times the simple gospel of Jesus to these Indians, and with so much success that some were ready to believe, but others doubted, just as in the days of old. For the benefit of the former, he had this day chosen the text, " Let us run with patience the race that is set before us, looking unto Jesus." Whitewing had been much troubled in spirit. His mind, if very inquiring, was also very sceptical. It was not that he would not—but that he could not—receive anything unless *convinced*. With a strong thirst after truth, he went to hear that day, but, strange to say, he could not fix his attention. Only one sentence seemed to fasten firmly on his memory : " It is the Spirit that quickeneth." The text itself also made a profound impression on him..

The preacher had just concluded, and was about to raise his voice in prayer, when a shout was heard in the distance. It came from a man who was seen running over the prairie towards the camp, with the desperate haste of one who runs for his life.

All was at once commotion. The men sprang up, and, while some went out to meet the runner, others seized their weapons. In a few seconds a young man with bloodshot eyes, labouring chest, and streaming brow burst into their midst, with the news that a band of Blackfoot warriors, many hundred strong, was on its way to attack the camp of Bald Eagle; that he was one of that old chief's braves, and was hasting to give his tribe timely warning, but that he had run so far and so fast as to be quite unable to go another step, and had turned aside to borrow a horse, or beg them to send on a fresh messenger.

"*I* will go," said Whitewing, on hearing this; "and my horse is ready."

He wasted no more time with words, but ran towards the hollow where his steed had been hobbled, that is, the two front legs tied together so as to admit of moderate freedom without the risk of desertion.

He was closely followed by his friend Little Tim, who, knowing well the red man's staid and self-possessed character, was somewhat surprised to see by his flashing eyes and quick breathing that he was unusually excited.

"Whitewing is anxious," he said, as they ran together.

"The woman whom I love better than life is in Bald Eagle's camp," was the brief reply.

"Oho!" thought Little Tim, but he spoke no word, for

he knew his friend to be extremely reticent in regard to matters of the heart. For some time he had suspected him of what he styled a weakness in that organ. "Now," thought he, "I know it."

"Little Tim will go with me?" asked the Indian, as they turned into the hollow where the horses had been left.

"Ay, Whitewing," answered the trapper, with a touch of enthusiasm; "Little Tim will stick to you through thick and thin, as long as——"

An exclamation from the Indian at that moment stopped him, for it was discovered that the horses were not there. The place was so open that concealment was not possible. The steeds of both men had somehow got rid of their hobbles and galloped away.

A feeling of despair came over the Indian at this discovery. It was quickly followed by a stern resolve. He was famed as being the fleetest and most enduring brave of his tribe. He would *run* home.

Without saying a word to his friend, he tightened his belt, and started off like a hound loosed from the leash. Little Tim ran a few hundred yards after him at top speed, but suddenly pulled up.

"Pooh! It's useless," he exclaimed. "I might as well run after a streak o' greased lightnin'. Well, well, women have much to answer for! Who'd iver have thowt to see Whitewing shook off his balance like that?

It strikes me I'll sarve him best by lookin' after the nags."

While the trapper soliloquised thus he ran back to the camp to get one of the Indian horses, wherewith to go off in search of his own and that of his friend. He found the Indians busy making preparations to ride to the rescue of their Bald Eagle allies; but quick though these sons of the prairie were, they proved too slow for Little Tim, who leaped on the first horse he could lay hold of, and galloped away.

Meanwhile Whitewing ran with the fleet, untiring step of a trained runner whose heart is in his work; but the way was long, and as evening advanced even his superior powers began to fail a little. Still he held on, greatly overtaxing his strength. Nothing could have been more injudicious in a prolonged race. He began to suspect that it was unwise, when he came to a stretch of broken ground, which in the distance was traversed by a range of low hills. As he reached these he reduced the pace a little, but while he was clambering up the face of a rather precipitous cliff, the thought of the Blackfoot band and of the much-loved one came into his mind; prudence went to the winds, and in a moment he was on the summit of the cliff, panting vehemently—so much so, indeed, that he felt it absolutely necessary to sit down for a few moments to rest.

While resting thus, with his back against a rock, in the attitude of one utterly worn out, part of the missionary's text flashed into his mind : "the race that is set before us."

"Surely," he murmured, looking up, "this race is set before me. The object is good. It is my duty as well as my desire."

The thought gave an impulse to his feelings ; the impulse sent his young blood careering, and, springing up, he continued to run as if the race had only just begun. But ere long the pace again began to tell, producing a sinking of the heart, which tended to increase the evil. Hour after hour had passed without his making any perceptible abatement in the pace, and the night was now closing in. This however mattered not, for the full moon was sailing in a clear sky, ready to relieve guard with the sun. Again the thought recurred that he acted unwisely in thus pressing on beyond his powers, and once more he stopped and sat down.

This time the text could not be said to flash into his mind, for while running, it had never left him. He now deliberately set himself to consider it, and the word "patience" arrested his attention.

"Let us run with patience," he thought. "I have not been patient. But the white man did not mean this kind of race at all ; he said it was the whole race of life.

Well, if so, *this* is part of that race, and it *is* set before
me. Patience! patience! I will try."

With childlike simplicity the red man rose and began
to run slowly. For some time he kept it up, but
as his mind reverted to the object of his race his
patience began to ooze out. He could calculate pretty
well the rate at which the Blackfoot foes would probably
travel, and knowing the exact distance, perceived that it
would be impossible for him to reach the camp before
them, unless he ran all the way at full speed. The very
thought of this induced him to put on a spurt, which
broke him down altogether. Stumbling over a piece of
rough ground, he fell with such violence that for a
moment or two he lay stunned. Soon, however, he
was on his legs again, and tried to resume his headlong
career, but felt that the attempt was useless. With a
deep irrepressible groan, he sank upon the turf.

It was in this hour of his extremity that the latter
part of the preacher's text came to his mind : "looking
unto Jesus."

Poor Whitewing looked upwards, as if he half expected
to see the Saviour with the bodily eye, and a mist seemed
to be creeping over him. He was roused from this semi-
conscious state by the clattering of horses' hoofs.

The Blackfoot band at once occurred to his mind.
Starting up, he hid behind a piece of rock. The sounds

drew nearer, and presently he saw horsemen passing him at a considerable distance. How many he could not make out. There seemed to be very few. The thought that it might be his friend the trapper occurred, but if he were to shout, and it should turn out to be foes, not only would his own fate but that of his tribe be sealed. The case was desperate; still, anything was better than remaining helplessly where he was. He uttered a sharp cry.

It was responded to at once in the voice of Little Tim, and next moment the faithful trapper galloped towards Whitewing leading his horse by the bridle.

"Well, now, this *is* good luck," cried the trapper, as he rode up.

"No," replied the Indian gravely, "it is not *luck.*"

"Well, as to that, I don't much care what you call it— but get up. Why, what's wrong wi' you?"

"The run has been very long, and I pressed forward impatiently, trusting too much to my own strength. Let my friend help me to mount."

"Well, now I come to think of it," said the trapper, as he sprang to the ground, "you *have* come a tremendous way—a most awful long way—in an uncommon short time. A fellow don't think o' that when he's mounted, ye see. There now," he added, resuming his own seat in the saddle, "off we go. But there's no need to overdrive the cattle ; we 'll be there in good time, I warrant ye, for the nags are both good and fresh."

Little Tim spoke the simple truth, for his own horse, which he had discovered along with that of his friend some time after parting from him, was a splendid animal, much more powerful and active than the ordinary Indian horses. The steed of Whitewing was a half-wild creature of Spanish descent, from the plains of Mexico.

Nothing more was spoken after this. The two horsemen rode steadily on side by side, proceeding with long but not too rapid strides over the ground : now descending into the hollows, or ascending the gentle undulations of the plains ; anon turning out and in to avoid the rocks and ruts and rugged places ; or sweeping to right or left to keep clear of clumps of stunted wood and thickets, but never for a moment drawing rein until the goal was reached, which happened very shortly before the break of day.

The riding was absolute rest to Whitewing, who recovered strength rapidly as they advanced.

"There is neither sight nor sound of the foe here," murmured the Indian.

"No, all safe !" replied the trapper in a tone of satisfaction, as they cantered to the summit of one of the prairie waves, and beheld the wigwams of Bald Eagle shining peacefully in the moonlight on the plain below.

CHAPTER II.

THE SURPRISE AND COMBAT.

HOW frequently that "slip 'twixt the cup and the lip" is observed in the affairs of this life! Little Tim, the trapper, had barely pronounced the words "All safe," when an appalling yell rent the air, and a cloud of dark forms was seen to rush over the open space that lay between the wigwams of the old chief Bald Eagle and a thicket that grew on its westward side.

The Blackfoot band had taken the slumbering Indians completely by surprise, and Whitewing had the mortification of finding that he had arrived just a few minutes too late to warn his friends. Although Bald Eagle was thus caught unprepared, he was not slow to meet the enemy. Before the latter had reached the village, all the fighting men were up, and armed with bows, scalping-knives, and tomahawks. They had even time to rush towards the foe, and thus prevent the fight from commencing in the midst of the village.

The world is all too familiar with the scenes that ensued. It is not our purpose to describe them. We detest war, regarding it in ninety-nine cases out of a hundred as unnecessary. Sufficient to say here that the over-whelming numbers of the Blackfoot Indians were too much for their enemies. They soon began to overpower and drive them back towards the wigwams, where the poor women and children were huddled together in terror.

Before this point had arrived, however, Whitewing and Little Tim were galloping to the rescue. The former knew at a glance that resistance on the part of his friends would be hopeless. He did not therefore gallop straight down to the field of battle to join them, but, turning sharply aside with his friend, swept along one of the bottoms or hollows between the undulations of the plain, where their motions could not be seen as they sped along. Whitewing looked anxiously at Little Tim, who, observing the look, said—

" I 'm with 'ee, Whitewing, niver fear."

" Does my brother know that we ride to death ?" asked the Indian in an earnest tone.

" Yer brother don't know nothin' o' the sort," replied the trapper, "and, considerin' your natur', I 'd have expected ye to think that Manitou might have *some* hand in the matter."

" The white man speaks wisely," returned the chief,

accepting the reproof with a humbled look. "We go in His strength."

And once again the latter part of the preacher's text seemed to shoot through the Indian's brain like a flash of light—"looking unto Jesus."

Whitewing was one of those men who are swift to conceive and prompt in action. Tim knew that he had a plan of some sort in his head, and, having perfect faith in his capacity, forbore to advise him, or even to speak. He merely drew his hunting-knife, and urged his steed to its utmost speed, for every moment of time was precious. The said hunting-knife was one of which Little Tim was peculiarly fond. It had been presented to him by a Mexican general for conspicuous gallantry in saving the life of one of his officers in circumstances of extreme danger. It was unusually long and heavy, and, being double-edged, bore some resemblance to the short sword of the ancient Romans.

"It'll do some execution before I go down," thought Tim, as he regarded the bright blade with an earnest look.

But Tim was wrong. The blade was not destined to be tarnished that day.

In a very few minutes the two horsemen galloped round to the thicket which had concealed the enemy. Entering this they dashed through it as fast as possible

B

until they reached the other side, whence they could see
the combatants on the plain beyond.   All along they
had heard the shouts and yells of battle.

For one moment Whitewing drew up to breathe his
gallant steed, but the animal was roused by that time, and
it was difficult to restrain him.   His companion's horse
was also nearly unmanageable.

"My brother's voice is strong.   Let him use it well,"
said the chief abruptly.

" Ay, ay," replied the little trapper, with an intelligent
chuckle; " go ahead, my boy.   I 'll give it out fit to bu'st
the bellows."

Instantly Whitewing shot from the wood, like the
panther rushing on his prey, uttering at the same time
the tremendous warcry of his tribe.   Little Tim followed
suit with a roar that was all but miraculous in its tone
and character, and may be described as a compound of
the steam-whistle and the buffalo-bull, only with something about it intensely human.   It rose high above the
din of battle.   The combatants heard and paused.   The
two horsemen were seen careering towards them with
furious gesticulations.   Red Indians seldom face certain
death.   The Blackfoot men knew that an attack by only
two men would be sheer insanity; the natural conclusion
was that they were the leaders of a band just about to
emerge from the thicket.   They were thus taken in rear.

A panic seized them, which was intensified when Little Tim repeated his roar and flourished the instrument of death, which he styled his "little carving-knife." The Blackfeet turned and fled right and left, scattering over the plains individually and in small groups, as being the best way of baffling pursuit.

With that sudden access of courage which usually results from the exhibition of fear in a foe, Bald Eagle's men yelled and gave chase. Bald Eagle himself, however, had the wisdom to call them back.

At a council of war, hastily summoned on the spot, he said—

"My braves, you are a parcel of fools."

Clearing his throat after this plain statement, either for the purpose of collecting his thoughts or giving his young warriors time to weigh and appreciate the compliment, he continued—

"You chase the enemy as thoughtlessly as the north wind chases the leaves in autumn. My wise chief Whitewing, and his friend Leetil Tim—whose heart is big, and whose voice is bigger, and whose scalping-knife is biggest of all—have come to our rescue *alone*. White-wing tells me there is no one at their backs. If our foes discover their mistake, they will turn again, and the contempt which they ought to pour on themselves because of their own cowardice they will heap on *our* heads, and overwhelm us by their numbers—for who can withstand numbers? They will scatter us like small dust before the hurricane. Waugh!"

The old man paused for breath, for the recent fight had taken a good deal out of him, and the assembled warriors exclaimed "Waugh!" by which they meant to express entire approval of his sentiments. "Now it is my counsel," he continued, "that as we have been saved by Whitewing, we should all shut our mouths, and hear what Whitewing has got to say."

Bald Eagle sat down amid murmurs of applause, and Whitewing arose.

There was something unusually gentle in the tone and aspect of the young chief on this occasion.

"Our father, the ancient one who has just spoken words of wisdom," he said, stretching forth his right hand, "has told you the truth, yet not quite the truth. He is right when he says that Leetil Tim and I have come to your rescue, but he is wrong when he says we come alone. It is true that there are no men at our backs to help us, but is not Manitou behind us—in front —around? It was Manitou who sent us here, and it was He who gave us the victory."

Whitewing paused, and there were some exclamations of approval, but they were not so numerous or so decided as he could have wished, for red men are equally unwilling with white men to attribute their successes directly to their Creator.

"And now," he continued, "as Bald Eagle has said, if our foes find out their mistake, they will, without doubt, return. We must therefore take up our goods, our wives, and our little ones, and hasten to meet our brothers of Clearvale, who are even now on their way to help us. Our band is too small to fight the Blackfeet, but united with our friends, and with Manitou on our side for our cause is just, we shall be more than a match for them. I counsel, then, that we raise the camp without delay."

The signs of approval were much more decided at the close of this brief address, and the old chief again rose up.

"My braves," he said, "have listened to the words of wisdom. Let each warrior go to his wigwam and get ready. We quit the camp when the sun stands *there.*"

He pointed to a spot in the sky where the sun would be shining about an hour after daybreak, which was already brightening the eastern sky.

As he spoke the dusky warriors seemed to melt from the scene as if by magic, and ere long the whole camp was busy packing up goods, catching horses, fastening on dogs little packages suited to their size and strength, and otherways making preparation for immediate departure.

"Follow me," said Whitewing to Little Tim, as he turned like the rest to obey the orders of the old chief.

"Ay, it's time to be lookin' after *her*," said Tim, with something like a wink of one eye, but the Indian was too much occupied with his own thoughts to observe the act or appreciate the allusion. He strode swiftly through the camp.

"Well, well," soliloquised the trapper as he followed, "I niver did expect to see Whitewing in this state o' mind. He's or'narily sitch a cool, unexcitable man. Ah! women, you've much to answer for!"

Having thus apostrophised the sex, he hurried on in silence, leaving his horse to the care of a youth, who also took charge of Whitewing's steed.

Close to the outskirts of the camp stood a wigwam somewhat apart from the rest. It belonged to Whitewing. Only two women were in it at the time the young Indian chief approached. One was a good-looking young girl, whose most striking feature was her large, earnest-looking, dark eyes. The other was a wrinkled old woman, who might have been any age between fifty and a hundred, for a life of exposure and hardship, coupled with a somewhat delicate constitution, had dried her up to such an extent that, when asleep, she might easily have passed for an Egyptian mummy. One redeeming point in the poor old thing was the fact that all the deep wrinkles in her

"THE OTHER WAS A WRINKLED OLD WOMAN."—Page 22.

weather-worn and wigwam-smoked visage ran in the lines of kindliness. Her loving character was clearly stamped upon her mahogany countenance, so that he who ran might easily read.

With the characteristic reserve of the red man, White-wing merely gave the two women a slight look of recognition, which was returned with equal quietness by the young woman, but with a marked rippling of the wrinkles on the part of the old. There still remained a touch of anxiety caused by the recent fight on both countenances. It was dispelled, however, by a few words from Whitewing, who directed the younger woman to prepare for instant flight. She acted with prompt, unquestioning obedience, and at the same time the Indian went to work to pack up his goods with all speed. Of course Tim lent efficient aid to tie up the packs and prepare them for slinging on horse and dog.

"I say, Whitewing," whispered Tim, touching the chief with his elbow, and glancing at the young woman with approval—for Tim, who was an affectionate fellow and anxious about his friend's welfare, rejoiced to observe that the girl was obedient and prompt as well as pretty —"I say, is that *her ?*"

Whitewing looked with a puzzled expression at his friend.

"Is that *her—the* girl, you know?" said Little Tim,

with a series of looks and nods which were intended to convey worlds of deep meaning.

"She is my sister—Brighteyes," replied the Indian quietly, as he continued his work.

"Whew!" whistled the trapper. "Well, well," he murmured in an undertone, "you're on the wrong scent this time altogether, Tim. Ye think yerself a mighty deal cliverer than ye are. Niver mind, the one that he says he loves more nor life'll turn up soon enough, no doubt. But I'm real sorry for the old 'un," he added in an undertone, casting a glance of pity on the poor creature, who bent over the little fire in the middle of the tent, and gazed silently yet inquiringly at what was going on. "She'll niver be able to stand a flight like this. The mere joltin' o' the nags 'ud shake her old bones a'most out of her skin. There are *some* Redskins, now, that would leave her to starve, but Whitewing'll niver do that. I know him better. Now then"—aloud— "have ye anything more for me to do?"

"Let my brother help Brighteyes to bring up and pack the horses."

"Jist so. Come along, Brighteyes."

With the quiet promptitude of one who has been born and trained to obey, the Indian girl followed the trapper out of the wigwam.

Being left alone with the old woman, some of the

young chief's reserve wore off, though he did not descend to familiarity.

"Mother," he said, sitting down beside her and speaking loud, for the old creature was rather deaf, "we must fly. The Blackfeet are too strong for us. Are you ready?"

"I am always ready to do the bidding of my son," replied this pattern mother. "But sickness has made me old before my time. I have not strength to ride far. Manitou thinks it time for me to die. It is better for Whitewing to leave me and give his care to the young ones."

"The young ones can take care of themselves," replied the chief somewhat sternly. "We know not what Manitou thinks. It is our business to live as long as we can. If you cannot ride, mother, I will carry you. Often you have carried *me* when I could not ride."

It is difficult to guess why Whitewing dropped his poetical language, and spoke in this matter-of-fact and sharp manner. Great thoughts had been swelling in his bosom for some time past, and perchance he was affected by the suggestion that the cruel practice of deserting the aged was not altogether unknown in his tribe. It may be that the supposition of his being capable of such cruelty nettled him. At all events, he said nothing more except to tell his mother to be ready to start at once.

The old woman herself, who seemed to be relieved that her proposition was not favourably received, began to obey her son's directions by throwing a gay-coloured handkerchief over her head, and tying it under her chin. She then fastened her moccasins more securely on her feet, wrapped a woollen kerchief round her shoulders, and drew a large green blanket around her, strapping it to her person by means of a broad strip of deerskin. Having made these simple preparations for whatever journey lay before her, she warmed her withered old hands over the embers of the wood fire, and awaited her son's pleasure.

Meanwhile that son went outside to see the preparations for flight carried into effect.

" We 're all ready," said Little Tim, whom he met not far from the wigwam. " Horses and dogs down in the hollow ; Brighteyes an' a lot o' youngsters lookin' after them. All you want now is to get hold o' *her*, and be off; an' the sooner the better, for Blackfoot warriors don't take long to get over scares an' find out mistakes. But I 'm most troubled about the old woman. She 'll niver be able to stand it."

To this Whitewing paid little attention. In truth, his mind seemed to be taken up with other thoughts, and his friend was not much surprised, having come, as we have seen, to the conclusion that the Indian was under a temporary spell for which woman was answerable.

"Is my horse at hand?" asked Whitewing.

"Ay, down by the creek, all ready."

"And my brother's horse?"

"Ready too, at the same place; but we 'll want another good 'un—for *her*, you know," said Tim suggestively.

"Let the horses be brought to my wigwam," returned Whitewing, either not understanding or disregarding the last remark.

The trapper was slightly puzzled, but, coming to the wise conclusion that his friend knew his own affairs best, and had, no doubt, made all needful preparations, he went off quietly to fetch the horses, while the Indian returned to the wigwam. In a few minutes Little Tim stood before the door, holding the bridles of the two horses.

Immediately afterwards a little Indian boy ran up with a third and somewhat superior horse, and halted beside him.

"Ha! that 's it at last. The horse for *her*," said the trapper to himself with some satisfaction; "I knowed that Whitewing would have everything straight—even though he *is* in a raither stumped condition just now."

As he spoke, Brighteyes ran towards the wigwam, and

looked in at the door. Next moment she went to the steed which Little Tim had, in his own mind, set aside for "*her*," and vaulted into the saddle as a young deer might have done had it taken to riding.

Of course Tim was greatly puzzled, and forced to admit a second time that he had over-estimated his own cleverness, and was again off the scent. Before his mind had a chance of being cleared up, the skin curtain of the wigwam was raised, and Whitewing stepped out with a bundle in his arms. He gave it to Little Tim to hold while he mounted his somewhat restive horse, and then the trapper became aware—from certain squeaky sounds, and a pair of eyes that glittered among the folds of the bundle—that he held the old woman in his arms!

"I say, Whitewing," he said remonstratively, as he handed up the bundle, which the Indian received tenderly in his left arm, "most o' the camp has started. In quarter of an hour or so there 'll be none left. Don't 'ee think it 's about time to look after *her?*"

Whitewing looked at the trapper with a perplexed expression—a look which did not quite depart after his friend had mounted, and was riding through the half-deserted camp beside him.

"Now, Whitewing," said the trapper, with some decision of tone and manner, "I 'm quite as able as you are to carry that old critter. If you 'll make her over to me, you'll be better able to look after *her*, you know. Eh?"

"My brother speaks strangely to-day," replied the chief. "His words are hidden from his Indian friend. What does he mean by '*her*'?"

"Well, well, now, ye *are* slow," answered Tim; "I wouldn't ha' believed that anything short o' scalpin' could ha' took away yer wits like that. Why, of course I mean the woman ye said was dearer to 'ee than life."

"That woman is here," replied the chief gravely, casting a brief glance down at the wrinkled old visage that nestled upon his breast—"my mother."

"Whew!" whistled the trapper, opening his eyes very wide indeed. For the third time that day he was constrained to admit that he had been thrown completely off the scent, and that, in regard to cleverness, he was no better than a "squawkin' babby."

But Little Tim said never a word. Whatever his thoughts might have been after that, he kept them to himself, and, imitating his Indian brother, maintained profound silence as he galloped between him and Bright-eyes over the rolling prairie.

CHAPTER III.

THE MASSACRE AND THE CHASE.

THE sun was setting when Whitewing and his friends rode into Clearvale. The entrance to the valley was narrow, and for a short distance the road, or Indian track, wound among groups of trees and bushes which effectually concealed the village from their sight.

At this point in the ride Little Tim began to recover from the surprise at his own stupidity which had for so long a period of time reduced him to silence. Riding up alongside of Whitewing, who was a little in advance of the party, still bearing his mother in his arms, he accosted him thus—

"I say, Whitewing, the longer I know you, the more of a puzzle you are to me. I thowt I'd got about at the bottom o' all yer notions an' ways by this time, but I find that I'm mistaken."

As no question was asked, the red man deemed no reply needful, but the faintest symptom of a smile told the trapper that his remark was understood and appreciated.

"One thing that throws me off the scent," continued Little Tim, "is the way you Injins have got o' holdin' yer tongues, so that a feller can't make out what yer minds are after. Why don't you speak? why ain't you more commoonicative?"

"The children of the prairie think that wisdom lies in silence," answered Whitewing gravely. "They leave it to their women and white brothers to chatter out all their minds."

"Humph! The children o' the prairie ain't complimentary to their white brothers," returned the trapper. "Mayhap yer right. Some of us do talk a leetle too much. It 's a way we 've got o' lettin' off the steam. I 'm afeard I 'd bust sometimes if I didn't let my feelin's off through my mouth. But your silent ways are apt to lead fellers off on wrong tracks when there 's no need to. Didn't I think, now, that you was after a young woman as ye meant to take for a squaw—and after all it turned out to be your mother!"

"My white brother sometimes makes mistakes," quietly remarked the Indian.

"True; but your white brother wouldn't have made the mistake if ye had told him who it was you were after when ye set off like a mad grizzly wi' its pups in

C

danger. Didn't I go tearin' after you neck and crop as if I was a boy o' sixteen, in the belief that I was helpin' ye in a love affair?"

"It *was* a love affair," said the Indian quietly.

"True, but not the sort o' thing that I thowt it was."

"Would you have refused to help me if you had known better?" demanded Whitewing somewhat sharply.

"Nay, I won't say that," returned Tim, "for I hold that a woman's a woman, be she old or young, pretty or ugly, an' I'd scorn the man as would refuse to help her in trouble; besides, as the wrinkled old critter is *your* mother, I've got a sneakin' sort o' fondness for her; but if I'd only known, a deal o' what they call romance would ha' bin took out o' the little spree."

"Then it is well that my brother did *not* know."

To this the trapper merely replied "Humph!"

After a few minutes he resumed in a more confidential tone—

"But I say, Whitewing, has it niver entered into your head to take to yourself a wife? A man's always the better of havin' a female companion to consult with an' talk over things, you know, as well as to make his moccasins and leggin's."

"Does Little Tim act on his own opinions?" asked the Indian quickly.

"Ha! that's a fair slap in the face," said Tim, with a

laugh, " but there may be reasons for that, you see. Gals ain't always as willin' as they should be; sometimes they don't know a good man when they see him. Besides, I ain't too old yet, though p'raps some of 'em thinks me raither short for a husband. Come now, don't keep yer old comrade in the dark. Haven't ye got a notion o' some young woman in partikler ?"

" Yes," replied the Indian gravely.

" Jist so ; I thowt as much," returned the trapper, with a tone and look of satisfaction. " What may her name be ?"

" Lightheart."

" Ay ? Lightheart. A good name—specially if she takes after it, as I 've no doubt she do. An' what tribe does—— "

The trapper stopped abruptly, for at that moment the cavalcade swept out of the thicket into the open valley, and the two friends suddenly beheld the Indian camp, which they had so recently left, reduced to a smoking ruin.

It is impossible to describe the consternation of the Indians, who had ridden so far and so fast to join their friends. And how shall we speak of the state of poor Whitewing's feelings ? No sound escaped his compressed lips, but a terrible light seemed to gleam from his dark eyes, as, clasping his mother convulsively to his breast with his left arm, he grasped his tomahawk, and urged his horse to its utmost speed. Little Tim was at his side in a moment, with the long dagger flashing in his right hand, while Bald Eagle and his dusky warriors pressed close behind.

The women and children were necessarily left in the rear; but Whitewing's sister, Brighteyes, being better mounted than these, kept up with the men of war.

The scene that presented itself when they reached the camp was indeed terrible. Many of the wigwams were burned, some of them still burning, and those that had escaped the fire had been torn down and scattered about, while the trodden ground and pools of blood told of the dreadful massacre that had so recently taken place. It was evident that the camp had been surprised, and probably all the men slain, while a very brief examination sufficed to show that such of the women and children as were spared had been carried off into slavery. In every direction outside the camp were found the scalped bodies of the slain, left as they had fallen in unavailing defence of home.

The examination of the camp was made in hot haste and profound silence, because instant action had to be taken for the rescue of those who had been carried away, and Indians are at all times careful to restrain and hide their feelings. Only the compressed lip, the heaving bosom, the expanding nostrils, and the scowling eyes told of the fires that raged within.

In this emergency Bald Eagle, who was getting old and rather feeble, tacitly gave up the command of the braves to Whitewing. It need scarcely be said that the young chief acted with vigour. He with the trapper having traced the trail of the Blackfoot war-party—evidently a different band from that which had attacked Bald Eagle's camp—and ascertained the direction they had taken, divided his force into two bands, in command of which he placed two of the best chiefs of his tribe. Bald Eagle himself agreed to remain with a small force to protect the women and children. Having made his dispositions and given his orders, Whitewing mounted his horse, and galloped a short distance on the enemy's trail, followed by his faithful friend. Reining up suddenly, he said—

"What does my brother counsel?"

"Well, Whitewing, since ye ask, I would advise you to follow yer own devices. You've got a good head on your shoulders, and know what's best."

"Manitou knows what is best," said the Indian solemnly. "He directs *all*. But His ways are very dark. Whitewing cannot understand them."

"Still, we must act, you know," suggested the trapper.

"Yes, we must act; and I ask counsel of my brother, because it may be that Manitou shall cause wisdom and light to flow from the lips of the white man."

"Well, I don't know as to that, Whitewing, but my advice, whatever it's worth, is, that we should try to fall on the reptiles in front and rear at the same time, and that you and I should go out in advance to scout."

"Good," said the Indian; "my plan is so arranged."

Without another word he gave the rein to his impatient horse, and was about to set off at full speed, when he was arrested by the trapper exclaiming, "Hold on! here's some one coming after us."

A rider was seen galloping from the direction of the burned camp. It turned out to be Brighteyes.

"What brings my sister?" demanded Whitewing.

The girl with downcast look modestly requested leave to accompany them.

Her brother sternly refused. "It is not woman's part to fight," he said.

"True, but woman sometimes helps the fighter," replied the girl, not venturing to raise her eyes.

"Go," returned Whitewing. "Time may not be foolishly wasted. The old ones and the children need thy care."

Without a word Brighteyes turned her horse's head towards the camp, and was about to ride humbly away when Little Tim interfered.

"Hold on, girl! I say, Whitewing, she's not so far wrong. Many a time has woman rendered good service in warfare. She's well mounted, and might ride back with a message or something o' that sort. You'd better let her come."

"She may come," said Whitewing, and next moment he was bounding over the prairie at the full speed of his fiery steed, closely followed by Little Tim and Bright-eyes.

That same night, at a late hour, a band of savage warriors entered a thicket on the slopes of one of those hills on the western prairies which form what are some-times termed the spurs of the Rocky Mountains, though there was little sign of the great mountain range itself, which was still distant several days' march from the spot. A group of wearied women and children, some riding, some on foot, accompanied the band. It was that which had so recently destroyed the Indian village. They had pushed on with their prisoners and booty as far and as fast as their jaded horses could go, in order to avoid pursuit—though, having slain all the fighting men, there was little chance of that, except in the case of friends coming to the rescue, which they thought improbable. Still, with the wisdom of savage warriors, they took every precaution to guard against surprise. No fire was lighted in the camp, and sentries were placed all round it to guard them during the few hours they meant to devote to much-needed repose.

While these Blackfeet were eating their supper, Whitewing and Little Tim came upon them. Fortunately the sharp and practised eyes and intellects of our two friends were on the alert. So small a matter as a slight wavering in the Blackfoot mind as to the best place for encamping produced an effect on the trail sufficient to be instantly observed.

"H'm! they've took it into their heads here," said Little Tim, "that it might be advisable to camp an' feed."

Whitewing did not speak at once, but his reining up at the moment his friend broke silence showed that he too had observed the signs.

"It's always the way," remarked the trapper with a quiet chuckle as he peered earnestly at the ground which the moon enabled him to see distinctly, "if a band o' men only mention campin' when they're on the march they're sure to waver a bit an' spoil the straight, go-ahead run o' the trail."

"One turned aside to examine yonder bluff," said the Indian, pointing to a trail which he saw clearly, although it was undistinguishable to ordinary vision.

"Ay, an' the bluff didn't suit," returned Tim, "for here he rejoins his friends, an' they go off agin at the run. No more waverin'. They'd fixed their eyes a good bit ahead, an' made up their minds."

"They are in the thicket yonder," said the Indian, pointing to the place referred to.

"Jist what I was goin' to remark," observed the trapper. "Now, Whitewing, it behoves us to be cautious. Ay, I see your mind an' mine always jumps togither."

This latter remark had reference to the fact that the Indian had leaped off his horse and handed the reins to Brighteyes. Placing his horse also in charge of the Indian girl, Tim said, as the two set off—

"We have to do the rest on fut, an' the last part on our knees."

By this the trapper meant that he and his friend would have to creep up to the enemy's camp on hands and knees, but Whitewing, whose mind had been recently so much exercised on religious matters, at once thought of what he had been taught about the importance of prayer, and again the words "looking unto Jesus" rushed with greater power than ever upon his memory, so that, despite his anxiety as to the fate of his affianced bride and the perilous nature of the enterprise in hand, he kept puzzling his inquiring brain with such difficulties as the absolute dependence of man on the will and leading of God, coupled with the fact of his being required to go into vigorous, decisive, and apparently independent action, trusting entirely to his own resources.

"Mystery," thought the red man, as he and his

friend walked swiftly along, taking advantage of the shelter afforded by every glade, thicket, or eminence; "all is mystery!"

But Whitewing was wrong, as many men in all ages have been on first bending their minds to the consideration of spiritual things. All is *not* mystery. In the dealings of God with man, much, very much, is mysterious, and by us in this life apparently insoluble; but many things—especially those things that are of vital importance to the soul—are as clear as the sun at noonday. However, our red man was at this time only beginning to run the spiritual race, and, like many others, he was puzzled.

But no sign did he show of what was going on within, as he glided along, bending his keen eyes intently on the Blackfoot trail.

At last they came to the immediate neighbourhood of the spot where it was rightly conjectured the enemy lay concealed. Here, as Tim had foretold, they went upon their knees, and advanced with the utmost caution. Coming to a grassy eminence they lay flat down and worked their way slowly and painfully to the top.

Well was it for them that a few clouds shrouded the moon at that time, for one of the Blackfoot sentinels had been stationed on that grassy eminence, and if Whitewing and the trapper had been less expert in the arts of savage war, they must certainly have been discovered. As it was, they were able to draw off in time and reach another part of the mound where a thick bush effectually concealed them from view.

From this point, when the clouds cleared away, the camp could be clearly seen in the vale below. Even the forms of the women and children were distinguishable, but not their faces.

"It won't be easy to get at them by surprise," whis-pered the trapper. "Their position is strong, and they keep a bright lookout; besides, the moon won't be down for some hours yet—not much before daybreak."

"Whitewing will take the prey from under their very noses," returned the Indian.

"That won't be easy, but I've no doubt you'll try; an' sure, Little Tim's the man to back ye, anyhow."

At that moment a slight rustling noise was heard. Looking through the bush, they saw the Blackfoot sentinel approaching. Instantly they sank down into the grass, where they lay so flat and still that it seemed as if they had vanished entirely from the scene.

When the sentinel was almost abreast of them, a sound arose from the camp which caused him to stop and listen. It was the sound of song. The missionary—the only *man* the Blackfoot Indians had not slain—having finished supper, had gathered some of the women and children round him, and, after an earnest prayer, had begun a hymn of praise.   At first the Blackfoot chief was on the point of ordering them to cease, but as the sweet notes arose he seemed to be spell-bound, and remained a silent and motionless listener.   The sentinel on the mound also became like a dark statue.   He had never heard such tones before.

After listening a few minutes in wonder, he walked slowly to the end of the mound nearest to the singers.

"Now's our chance, Whitewing," said the trapper, rising from his lair.

The Indian made no reply, but descended the slope as carefully as he had ascended it, followed by his friend. In a short time they were back at the spot where the horses had been left in charge of Brighteyes.

Whitewing took his sister aside, and for a few minutes they conversed in low tones.

"I have arranged it all with Brighteyes," said the Indian, returning to the trapper.

"Didn't I tell 'ee," said Tim, with a low laugh, "that women was good at helpin' men in time o' war ?   Depend upon it that the sex must have a finger in every pie; and, moreover, the pie's not worth much that they haven't got a finger in."

To these remarks the young chief vouchsafed no

"THE SENTINEL ON THE MOUND ALSO BECAME LIKE A DARK STATUE."
—Page 44.

answer, but gravely went about making preparations to carry out his plans.

While tying the three horses to three separate trees, so as to be ready for instant flight, he favoured his friend with a few explanations.

" It is not possible," he said, " to take more than three just now, for the horses cannot carry more. But these three Brighteyes will rescue from the camp, and we will carry them off. Then we will return with our braves and save all the rest—if Manitou allows."

The trapper looked at his friend in surprise. He had never before heard him make use of such an expression as the last. Nevertheless, he made no remark, but while the three were gliding silently over the prairie again towards the Blackfoot camp he kept murmuring to himself: " You 're a great puzzle, Whitewing, an' I can't make ye out nohow. Yet I make no doubt yer right. Whativer ye do comes right somehow ; but yer a great puzzle—about the greatest puzzle that 's comed across my tracks since I was a squallin' little babby-boy !"

CHAPTER IV. -

CIRCUMVENTING THE BLACKFEET.

O N reaching the neighbourhood of the Blackfoot camp, Whitewing and his companions crept to the top of the eminence which overlooked it, taking care, however, to keep as far away as possible from the sentinel who still watched there.

Brighteyes proved herself to be quite as expert as her male companions in advancing like a snake through the long grass, though encumbered with a blanket wrapped round her shoulders. The use of this blanket soon became apparent. As the three lay prone on their faces looking down at the camp, from which the sound of voices still arose in subdued murmurs, the young chief said to his sister—

" Let the signal be a few notes of the song Brighteyes learned from the white preacher. Go."

Without a word of reply, the girl began to move gently forward, maintaining her recumbent position as she went, and gradually, as it were, melted away.

The moon was still shining brightly, touching every object with pale but effective lights, and covering hillocks and plains with correspondingly dark shadows. In a few minutes Brighteyes had crept past the young sentinel, and lay within sight—almost within earshot— of the camp.

Much to her satisfaction she observed that the Indians had not bound their captives. Even the missionary's hands were free. Evidently they thought, and were perhaps justified in thinking, that escape was impossible, for the horses of the party were all gathered together and hobbled, besides being under a strong guard; and what chance could women and children have, out on the plains on foot, against mounted men, expert to follow the faintest trail? As for the white man, he was a man of peace and unarmed, as well as ignorant of warriors' ways. The captives were therefore not only unbound, but left free to move about the camp at will, while some of their captors slept, some fed, and others kept watch.

The missionary had just finished singing a hymn, and was about to begin to read a portion of God's Word, when one of the women left the group, and wandered accidentally close to the spot where Brighteyes lay. It was Lightheart.

" Sister," whispered Brighteyes.

The girl stopped abruptly, and bent forward to listen,

D

with intense anxiety depicted on every feature of her pretty brown face.

"Sister," repeated Brighteyes, "sink in the grass and wait."

Lightheart was too well trained in Indian ways to speak or hesitate. At once, but slowly, she sank down and disappeared. Another moment, and Brighteyes was at her side.

"Sister," she said, "Manitou has sent help. Listen. We must be wise and quick."

From this point she went on to explain in as few words as possible that three fleet horses were ready close at hand to carry off three of those who had been taken captive, and that she, Lightheart, must be one of the three.

"But I cannot, will not, escape," said Lightheart, "while the others and the white preacher go into slavery."

To this Brighteyes replied that arrangements had been made to rescue the whole party, and that she and two others were merely to be, as it were, the firstfruits of the enterprise. Still Lightheart objected; but when her companion added that the plan had been arranged by her affianced husband, she acquiesced at once with Indian-like humility.

"I had intended," said Brighteyes, "to enter the Blackfoot camp as if I were one of the captives, and thus make known our plans ; but that is not now necessary. Lightheart will carry the news; she is wise, and knows how to act. Whitewing and Leetil Tim are hid on yonder hillock like snakes in the grass. I will return to them, and let Lightheart, when she comes, be careful to avoid the sentinel there———"

She stopped short, for at the moment a step was heard near them. It was that of a savage warrior, whose sharp eye had observed Lightheart quit the camp, and who had begun to wonder why she did not return.

In another instant Brighteyes flung her blanket round her, whispered to her friend, "Lie close," sprang up, and, brushing swiftly past the warrior with a light laugh—as though amused at having been discovered—ran into camp, joined the group round the missionary, and sat down. Although much surprised, the captives were too wise to express their feelings. Even the missionary knew enough of Indian tactics to prevent him from committing himself. He calmly continued the reading in which he had been engaged, and the Blackfoot warrior returned to his place, congratulating himself, perhaps, on having interrupted the little plan of one intending runaway.

Meanwhile Lightheart, easily understanding her friend's motives, crept in a serpentine fashion to the hillock, where she soon found Whitewing—to the intense but unexpressed joy of that valiant red man.

"Will Leetil Tim go back with Lightheart to the horses and wait, while his brother remains here?" said the young chief.

"No, Little Tim *won't*," growled the trapper, in a tone of decision that surprised his red friend. "Brighteyes is in the Blackfoot camp," he continued, in growling explanation.

"True," returned the Indian, "but Brighteyes will escape; and even if she fails to do so now, she will be rescued with the others at last."

"She will be rescued with *us*, just *now*," returned Little Tim in a tone so emphatic that his friend looked at him with an expression of surprise that was unusually strong for a red-skin warrior. Suddenly a gleam of intelligence broke from his black eyes, and with the soft exclamation "Wah!" he sank flat on the grass again, and remained perfectly still.

Brighteyes found that it was not all plain sailing when she had mingled with her friends in the camp. In the first place, the missionary refused absolutely to quit the captives. He would remain with them, he said, and await God's will and leading. In the second place, no third person had been mentioned by her brother, whose chief anxiety had been for his bride and the white man, and it did not seem to Brighteyes creditable to quit the camp after all her risk and trouble without some trophy of her prowess. In this dilemma she put to herself the question, " Whom would Lightheart wish me to rescue ?"

Now, there were two girls among the captives, one of whom was a bosom friend of Lightheart; the other was a younger sister. To these Brighteyes went, and straightway ordered them to prepare for flight. They were of course quite ready to obey. All the preparation needed was to discard the blankets which Indian women are accustomed to wear as convenient cloaks by day. Thus unhampered, the two girls wandered about the camp, as several of the others had occasionally been doing. Separating from each other, they got into the outskirts in different directions. Meanwhile a hymn had been raised, which facilitated their plans by attracting the attention of the savage warriors. High above the rest, in one prolonged note, the voice of Brighteyes rang out like a silver flute.

"There's the signal," said Little Tim, as the sweet note fell on his listening ear.

Rising as he spoke, the trapper glided in a stooping posture down the side of the hillock, and round the base of it, until he got immediately behind the youthful sentinel. Then lying down, and creeping towards him with the utmost caution, he succeeded in getting so near that he could almost touch him. With one cat-like bound, Little Tim was on the Indian's back, and had him in his arms, while his broad horny hand covered his mouth, and his powerful forefinger and thumb grasped him viciously by the nose.

It was a somewhat curious struggle that ensued. The savage was much bigger than the trapper, but the trapper was much stronger than the savage. Hence the latter made fearful and violent efforts to shake the former off; while the former made not less fearful, though seemingly not quite so violent, efforts to hold on. The red man tried to bite, but Tim's hand was too broad and hard to be bitten. He tried to shake his nose free, but unfortunately his nose was large, and Tim's grip of it was perfect. The savage managed to get just enough of breath through his mouth to prevent absolute suffocation, but nothing more. He had dropped his tomahawk at the first onset, and tried to draw his knife, but Tim's arms were so tight round him that he could not get his hand to his back, where the knife reposed in his belt. In desperation he stooped forward, and tried to throw his enemy over his head; but Tim's legs were wound round him, and no limpet ever embraced a rock with greater tenacity than did Little Tim embrace that Blackfoot brave. Half choking and wholly maddened, the savage suddenly turned heels over head, and fell on Tim with a force that ought to have burst him. But Tim didn't burst! He was much too tough for that. He did not even complain!

Rising again, a sudden thought seemed to strike the Indian, for he began to run towards the camp with his foe on his back. But Tim was prepared for that. He untwined one leg, lowered it, and with an adroit twist tripped up the savage, causing him to fall on his face with tremendous violence. Before he could recover, Tim, still covering the mouth and holding tight to the nose, got a knee on the small of the savage's back and squeezed it smaller. At the same time he slid his left hand up to the savage's windpipe, and compressed it. With a violent heave, the Blackfoot sprang up. With a still more violent heave, the trapper flung him down, bumped his head against a convenient stone, and brought the combat to a sudden close. Without a moment's loss of time, Tim gagged and bound his adversary. Then he rose up with a deep inspiration, and wiped his forehead, as he contemplated him.

"All this comes o' your desire not to shed human blood, Whitewing," he muttered. "Well, p'raps you're right; what would ha' bin the use o' killin' the poor crittur? But it was a tough job!"—saying which, he lifted the Indian on his broad shoulders, and carried him away.

While this fight was thus silently going on, hidden from view of the camp by the hillock, Whitewing crept forward to meet Brighteyes and the two girls, and these, with Light heart, were eagerly awaiting the trapper. " My brother is strong," said Whitewing, allowing the faintest possible smile to play for a moment on his usually grave face.

" Your brother is tough," returned Little Tim, rubbing the back of his head with a rueful look; " an' he's bin bumped about an' tumbled on to that extent that it's a miracle a whole bone is left in his carcass. But lend a hand, lad; we've got no time to waste."

Taking the young Blackfoot between them, and followed by the silent girls, they soon reached the thicket, where the horses had been left. Here they bound their captive securely to a tree, and gave him a drink of water, with a knife pointed at his heart to keep him quiet, after which they re-gagged him. Then Whitewing led Lightheart through the thicket towards his horse, and took her up behind him. Little Tim took charge of Brighteyes. The young sister and the bosom friend mounted the third horse, and thus paired, they all galloped away.

But the work that our young chief had cut out for himself that night was only half accomplished. On reaching the rendezvous which he had appointed, he found the braves of his tribe impatiently awaiting him.

" My father sees that we have been successful," he said to Bald Eagle, who had been unable to resist the desire to ride out to the rendezvous with the fighting men. " The

"THEN WHITEWING LED LIGHTHEART THROUGH THE THICKET."—Page 56.

great Manitou has given us the victory thus far, as the white preacher said he would."

"My son is right. Whitewing will be a great warrior when Bald Eagle is in the grave. Go and conquer; I will return to camp with the women."

Thus relieved of his charge, Whitewing, who, however, had little desire to achieve the fame prophesied for him, proceeded to fulfil the prophecy to some extent. He divided his force into four bands, with which he galloped off towards the Blackfoot camp. On nearing it, he so arranged that they should attack the camp simultaneously at four opposite points. Little Tim commanded one of the bands, and he resolved in his own mind that his band should be the last to fall on the foe.

"Bloodshed *may* be avoided," he muttered to himself; "an' I hope it will, as Whitewing is so anxious about it. Anyhow, I'll do my best to please him."

Accordingly, on reaching his allotted position, Tim halted his men, and bided his time.

The moon still shone over prairie and hill, and not a breath of air stirred blade or leaf. All in nature was peace, save in the hearts of savage man. The Blackfoot camp was buried in slumber. Only the sentinels were on the alert. Suddenly one of these—like the war-horse, who is said to scent the battle from afar—pricked his ears, distended his nostrils, and listened. A low, muffled, thunderous sort of pattering on the plain in front. It might be a herd of buffaloes. The sentinel stood transfixed. The humps of buffaloes are large, but they do not usually attain to the size of men! The sentinel clapped his hand to his mouth, and gave vent to a yell which sent the blood spirting through the veins of all, and froze the very marrow in the bones of some! Prompt was the reply and turn-out of the Blackfoot warriors. Well used to war's alarms, there was no quaking in their bosoms. They were well named " braves."

But the noise in the camp prevented them from hearing or observing the approach of the enemy on the other side till almost too late. A whoop apprised the chief of the danger. He divided his forces, and lost some of his self-confidence.

"Here comes number three," muttered Little Tim, as he observed the third band emerge from a hollow on the left.

The Blackfoot chief observed it too, divided his forces again, and lost more of his self-confidence.

None of the three bands had as yet reached the camp, but they all came thundering down on it at the same time, and at the same whirlwind pace.

"Now for number four," muttered Little Tim. "Come, boys, an' at 'em!" he cried, unconsciously paraphrasing the Duke of Wellington's Waterloo speech.

At the same time he gave utterance to what he styled

a Rocky Mountain trapper's roar, and dashed forward in advance of his men, who, in trying to imitate the roar, intensified and rather complicated their own yell.

It was the last touch to the Blackfoot chief, who, losing the small remnant of his self-confidence, literally "sloped" into the long grass, and vanished, leaving his men to still further divide themselves, which they did effectually by scattering right and left like small-shot from a blunder-buss.

Great was the terror of the poor captives while this brief but decisive action lasted, for although they knew that the assailants were their friends, they could not be certain of the issue of the combat. Naturally, they crowded round their only male friend, the missionary.

"Do not fear," he said, in attempting to calm them ; "the good Manitou has sent deliverance. We will trust in Him."

The dispersion of their foes and the arrival of friends almost immediately followed these words. But the friends who arrived were few in number at first, for White-wing had given strict orders as to the treatment of the enemy. In compliance therewith, his men chased them about the prairie in a state of gasping terror ; but no weapon was used, and not a man was killed, though they were scattered beyond the possibility of reunion for at least some days to come.

Before that eventful night was over the victors were far from the scene of victory on their way home.

"It's not a bad style o' fightin'," remarked Little Tim to his friend as they rode away; "lots o' fun and fuss without much damage. Pity we can't do *all* our fightin' in that fashion."

"Waugh!" exclaimed Whitewing; but as he never explained what he meant by "waugh," we must leave it to conjecture. It is probable, however, that he meant assent, for he turned aside in passing to set free the Blackfoot who had been bound to a tree. That red man, having expected death, went off with a lively feeling of surprise, and at top speed, his pace being slightly accelerated by a shot—wide of the mark and at long range—from Little Tim.

Three weeks after these events a number of Indians were baptized by our missionary. Among them were the young chief Whitewing and Lightheart, and these two were immediately afterwards united in marriage. Next day the trapper, with much awkwardness and hesitation, requested the missionary to unite him and Brighteyes. The request was complied with, and thenceforward the white man and the red became more inseparable than ever. They hunted and dwelt together—to the ineffable joy of Whitewing's wrinkled old mother, whose youth seemed absolutely to revive under the influence of the high-pressure affection brought to bear on a colony of brown and whitey-brown grand-children by whom she was at last surrounded.

The doubts and difficulties of Whitewing were finally cleared away. He not only accepted fully the Gospel for himself, but became anxious to commend it to others as the only real and perfect guide in life and comfort in death. In the prosecution of his plans, he imitated the example of his "white father," roaming the prairie and the mountains far and wide with his friend the trapper, and even venturing to visit some of the lodges of his old foes the Blackfoot Indians, in his desire to run earnestly, yet with patience, the race that had been set before him—"looking unto Jesus."

Full twenty years rolled by, during which no record was kept of the sayings or doings of those whose fortunes we have followed thus far. At the end of that period, however, striking incidents in their career brought the most prominent among them again to the front—as the following chapters will show.

CHAPTER V.

THE MOUNTAIN FORTRESS.

IN one of those numerous narrow ravines of the Rocky Mountains which open out into the rolling prairies of the Saskatchewan there stood some years ago a log hut, or block-house, such as the roving hunters of the Far West sometimes erected as temporary homes during the inclement winter of those regions.

With a view to render the hut a castle of refuge as well as a home, its builder had perched it close to the edge of a nearly inaccessible cliff overhanging one of those brawling torrents which carry the melting snows of the great rocky range into one of the tributaries of the Saskatchewan river. On what may be called the land side of the hut there was a slight breastwork of logs. It seemed a weak defence truly, yet a resolute man with several guns and ammunition might have easily held it against a considerable band of savages.

One fine morning about the time when the leaves of

the forest were beginning to put on their gorgeous autumnal tints, a woman might have been seen ascending the zigzag path that led to the hut or fortress.

She was young, well formed, and pretty, and wore the Indian costume, yet there was something in her air and carriage, as well as the nut-brown colour of her hair, which told that either her father or her mother had been what the red men term a " pale-face."

With a light, bounding step, very different from that of the ordinary Indian squaw, she sprang from rock to rock as if in haste, and, climbing over the breastwork before mentioned, entered the hut.

The interior of the little fortress was naturally characteristic of its owner. A leathern capote and leggings hung from a nail in one corner; in another lay a pile of buffalo robes. The rough walls were adorned with antlers of the moose and other deer, from the various branches of which hung several powder-horns, fire-bags, and bullet-pouches. Near the rude fireplace, the chimney of which was plastered outside and in with mud, was a range of six guns, of various patterns and ages, all of which, being well polished and oiled, were evidently quite ready for instant service. Beside them hung an old cavalry sabre. Neither table nor chairs graced the simple mansion; but a large chest at one side served for the former, and doubtless contained the owner's

E

treasures, whatever these might be, while three rough stools, with only nine legs among them, did service for the latter.

The action of the young woman on entering was somewhat suggestive of the cause of her haste Without a moment's delay, she seized a powder-horn and bullet-pouch, and began to charge the guns, some with ball, others with slugs, as fast as she could. There was a cool, quiet celerity in her proceedings which proved that she was accustomed to the handling of such weapons.

No one looking upon the scene would have guessed that Softswan, as she was poetically named, was a bride, at that time in the midst of the honeymoon.

Yet such was the case. Her husband being the kindliest, stoutest, and handsomest fellow in all that region had won her heart and hand, had obtained her parents' consent, had been married in the nearest settlement by a travelling missionary, and had carried off his pretty bride to spend the honeymoon in his mountain fortress. We can scarcely call it his home, however, for it was only as we have said a temporary residence—the Rocky Mountains, from the Gulf of Mexico to the Arctic Circle, being his home.

While the Indian bride was engaged in charging the firearms, a rifle-shot was heard to echo among the surrounding cliffs. It was followed by a cry, as if some one had been wounded, and then there arose that terrible war-whoop of the red men which, once heard, can never be forgotten, and which inspires even the bravest with feelings of at least anxiety.

That Softswan was not free from alarm was pretty evident from the peculiar curl of her pretty eyebrows, but that the sounds did not unnerve her was also obvious from the quiet though prompt way in which she gathered up all the loaded firearms, and bore them swiftly to the breastwork in front of the cabin. Arranging the guns in a row at her side, so as to be handy, the girl selected one, laid it on the parapet, and carefully examined the priming. Having satisfied herself that it was all right, she cocked the piece, and quietly awaited the issue of events.

The weapon that Softswan had selected was not picked up at haphazard. It was deliberately chosen as being less deadly than the others, the charge being a few slugs or clippings of lead, which were not so apt to kill as rifle bullets; for Softswan, as her name might suggest, was gentle of spirit, and was influenced by none of that thirst for blood and revenge which characterised some of her Indian relatives.

After a time the poor girl's anxiety increased, for well she knew that a whoop and a cry such as she had heard were the sure precursors of something worse. Besides, she had seen the footprints of Blackfoot Indians in the valley below, and she knew from their appearance that those who had made them were on the war-path, in which circumstances savages usually dismiss any small amount of tender mercies with which they may have been naturally endowed.

"Oh why, why you's not come home, Big Tim?" she exclaimed at last, in broken English.

It may be well to explain at once that Big Tim, who was the only son of Little Tim, had such a decided pre-ference for the tongue of his white father, that he had taught it to his bride, and refused to converse with her in any other, though he understood the language of his mother Brighteyes quite as well as English.

If Big Tim had heard the pathetic question, he would have flown to the rescue more speedily than any other hunter of the Rocky Mountains, for he was the swiftest runner of them all; but unfortunately he was too far off at that moment to hear; not too far off, however, to hear the shot and cry which had alarmed his bride.

From the position which Softswan occupied she could see and command every portion of the zigzag approach to the hut, so that no one could reach her without being completely exposed to her fire if she were disposed to dispute the passage. As we have said, the hut stood on a cliff which overhung the torrent that brawled through the gorge, so that she was secure from attack in rear.

In a few minutes another rifle-shot was heard, and the war-whoop was repeated, this time much nearer than before.

With compressed lips and heightened colour, the solitary girl prepared to defend her castle. Presently she heard footsteps among the thick bushes below, as if of some one running in hot haste. Softswan laid her finger on the trigger, but carefully, for the advancing runner might be her husband. Oh why did he not shout to warn her? The poor girl trembled a little, despite her self-restraint, as she thought of the danger and the necessity for immediate action.

Suddenly the bushes on her left moved, and a man, pushing them aside, peeped from among them. He was a savage, in the war-paint and panoply of a Blackfoot brave. The spot to which he had crept was indeed the nearest to the hut that could be reached in that direction, but Softswan knew well that an impassable chasm separated her from the intruder, so she kept well concealed behind the breastwork, and continued to watch him through one of the peep-holes made in it for that purpose. She might have easily shot him, for he was within range, but her nature revolted from doing so, for he seemed to think that the hut was untenanted, and, instead of looking towards her place of concealment, leaned over the cliff so as to get a good view of the lower end of the zigzag track where it entered the woods.

Could he be a foe to the approaching Indians, or one of them ? thought the poor girl, rendered almost desperate by doubt and indecision.

Just then a man burst out of the woods below with a defiant shout, and sprang up the narrow track. It was Big Tim. The savage on the cliff pointed his rifle at him. Indecision, doubt, mercy were instantly swept away, and with the speed of the lightning flash the girl sent her charge of slugs into the savage. He collapsed, rolled over the cliff, and went crashing into the bushes underneath, but instantly sprang up, as if unhurt, and disappeared, just as a dozen of his comrades burst upon the scene from the woods below.

The echoing report of the gun and the fall of their companion evidently disconcerted the aim of the savages, for their scattering fire left the bounding Tim untouched. Before they could reload, Softswan sent them a present of another charge of slugs, which, the distance being great, so scattered itself as to embrace nearly the whole party, who thereupon went wounded and howling back into the forest.

"Well done, my soft one !" exclaimed Big Tim, as he took a flying leap over the low breastwork, and caught

"WELL DONE, MY SOFT ONE!"—Page 70.

his bride in his arms, for even in that moment of danger he could not help expressing his joy and thankfulness at finding her safe and well, when he had half expected to find her dead and scalped, if he found her at all.

Another moment, and he was kneeling at the breast-work, examining the firearms and ready for action.

"Fetch the sabre, my soft one," said Big Tim, addressing his bride by the title which he had bestowed on her on his wedding-day.

The tone in which he said this struck the girl as being unusually light and joyous, not quite in keeping with the circumstance of being attacked by overwhelming odds; but she was becoming accustomed to the eccentricities of her bold and stalwart husband, and had perfect confidence in him. Without, therefore, expressing surprise by word or look, she obeyed the order.

Unsheathing the weapon, the hunter felt its edge with his thumb, and a slight smile played on his features as he said—

"I have good news for the soft one to-day."

The soft one looked, but did not say, "Indeed, what is it?"

"Yes," continued the youth, sheathing the sabre; "the man with the kind heart and the snowy pinion has come back to the mountains. He will be here before the shadows of the trees grow much longer."

" Whitewing ? " exclaimed Softswan, with a gleam of pleasure in her bright black eyes.

" Just so. The prairie chief has come back to us, and is now a preacher."

" Has the pale-face preacher com' vis him ? " asked the bride, with a slightly troubled look, for she did not yet feel quite at home in her broken English, and feared that her husband might laugh at her mistakes, though nothing was further from the mind of the stout hunter than to laugh at his pretty bride. He did indeed sometimes indulge the propensity in that strange conventional region " his sleeve," but no owl of the desert was more solemn in countenance than Big Tim when Softswan perpetrated her lingual blunders.

" I know not," he replied, as he renewed the priming of one of the guns. " Hist! did you see something move under the willow bush yonder ? "

The girl shook her head.

" A rabbit, no doubt," said the hunter, lowering the rifle which he had raised, and resuming his easy uncon- cerned attitude, yet keeping his keen eye on the spot with a steadiness that showed his indifference was assumed.

" I know not whether the pale-face preacher is with him," he continued. " Those who told me about him could only say that a white man dressed like the crows was travelling a short distance in advance of Whitewing, but whether he was one of his party or not, they could not tell. Indeed it is said that Whitewing has no party with him, that he travels alone. If he does, he is more reckless than ever, seeing that his enemies the Blackfeet are on the war-path just now; but you never know what a half-mad redskin will do, and Whitewing is a queer customer."

Big Tim's style of speech was in accordance with his half-caste nature—sometimes flowing in channels of slightly poetic imagery, like that of his Indian mother; at other times dropping into the very matter-of-fact style of his white sire.

"Leetil Tim vill be glad," said Softswan.

"Ay, daddy will be pleased. By the way, I wonder what keeps him out so long? I half expected to find him here when I arrived. Indeed, I made sure it was him that tumbled yon Blackfoot off the cliff so smartly. You see, I didn't know you were such a plucky little woman, my soft one, though I might have guessed it, seeing that you possess all the good qualities under the sun; but a man hardly expects his squaw to be great on the war-path, d'ye see?"

Softswan neither smiled nor looked pleased at the compliment intended in these words.

"Me loves not to draw bloods," she said gravely, with a pensive look on the ground.

"Don't let that disturb you, soft one," said her husband, with a quiet laugh. "By the way he jumped after it I guess he has got no more harm than if you'd gin him an overdose o' physic. But them reptiles bein' in these parts makes me raither anxious about daddy. Did he say where he meant to hunt when he went off this morning?"

"Yes; Leetil Tim says hims go for hunt near Lipstock Hill."

"Just so; Lopstick Hill," returned Tim, correcting her with offhand gravity.

"But me hears a shote an' a cry," said the girl, with a suddenly anxious look.

"That was from one o' the redskins, whose thigh I barked for sendin' an arrow raither close to my head," said the young man.

"But," continued his bride, with increasing anxiety, "the shote an' the cry was long before you comes home. Pr'aps it bees Leetil Tim."

"Impossible," said Big Tim quickly; "father must have bin miles away at that time, for Lopstick Hill is good three hours' walk from here as the crow flies, an' the Blackfeet came from the opposite airt o' the compass."

The young hunter's prolonged silence after this, as well as the expression of his face, showed that he was not quite as easy in his mind as his words implied.

"Did the cry seem to be far off?" he asked at last quickly.

"Not far," returned his wife.

Without speaking, Big Tim began to buckle on the cavalry sabre, not in the loosely-swinging cavalry fashion, but closely and firmly to his side, with his broad waistbelt, so that it might not impede his movements. He then selected from the arms a short double-barrelled gun, and, slinging a powder-horn and shot-pouch over his shoulders, prepared to depart.

"Now listen, my soft one," he said, on completing his arrangements. "I feel a'most sartin sure that the cry ye heard was *not* daddy's; nevertheless, the bare possibility o' such a thing makes it my dooty to go an' see if it was the old man. I think the Blackfeet have drawed off to have a palaver, an' won't be back for a bit, so I'll jist slip down the precipice by our secret path; an' if they do come back when I'm away, pepper them well wi' slugs. I'll hear the shots, an' be back to you afore they can git up the hill. But if they should make a determined rush, don't you make too bold a stand agin 'em. Just let fly with the big bore when they're half-way up the track, an' then slip into the cave. I'll soon meet ye there, an we'll give the reptiles a surprise. Now, you'll be careful, soft one?"

Soft one promised to be careful, and Big Tim, entering

the hut, passed out at a back door, and descended the cliff to the torrent below by a concealed path which even a climbing monkey might have shuddered to attempt.

Meanwhile Softswan, re-arranging and re-examining her firearm, sat down behind the breastwork to guard the fort.

The sun was still high in the heavens, illuming a magnificent prospect of hill and dale and virgin forest, and glittering in the lakelets, pools, and rivers, which brightened the scene as far as the distant horizon, where the snow-clad peaks of the Rocky Mountains rose grandly into the azure sky.

The girl sat there almost motionless for a long time, exhibiting in her face and figure at once the keen watchfulness of the savage and the endurance of the pale-face.

Unlike many girls of her class, she had at one period been brought for a short time under the influence of men who loved the Lord Jesus Christ, and esteemed it equally a duty and a privilege to urge others to flee from the wrath to come and accept the Gospel offer of salvation—men who themselves had long before been influenced by the pale-face preacher to whom Softswan had already referred. The seed had, in her case, fallen into good ground, and had brought forth the fruit of an earnest desire to show good-will to all with whom she had to do. It had also aroused in her a hungering and thirsting for more knowledge of God and His ways.

It was natural, therefore, as she gazed on the splendid scene spread out before her, that the thoughts of this child of the backwoods should rise to contemplation of the Creator, and become less attentive to inferior matters than circumstances required.

She was recalled suddenly to the danger of her position by the appearance of a dark object, which seemed to crawl out of the bushes below, just where the zigzag track entered them. At the first glance it seemed to resemble a bear; a second and more attentive look suggested that it might be a man. Whether bear or man, however, it was equally a foe, at least so thought Softswan, and she raised one of the guns to her shoulder with a promptitude that would have done credit to Big Tim himself.

But she did not fire. The natural disinclination to shed blood restrained her—fortunately, as it turned out, —for the crawling object, on reaching the open ground, rose with apparent difficulty and staggered forward a few paces in what seemed to be the form of a drunken man. After one or two ineffectual efforts to ascend the track, the unfortunate being fell and remained a motionless heap upon the ground.

CHAPTER VI.

A STRANGE VISITOR.

A CURIOUS mingling of eagerness, hope, and fear
rendered Softswan for some minutes undecided
how to act as she gazed at the fallen man.   His garb was
of a dark uniform grey colour, which she had often heard
described, but had not seen until now.   That he was
wounded she felt quite sure, but she knew that there
would be great danger in descending to aid him.   Besides,
if he were helpless, as he seemed to be, she had not
physical strength to lift him, and would expose herself to
easy capture if the Blackfeet should be in ambush.

Still, the eager and indefinable hope that was in her
heart induced the girl to rise with the intention of
descending the path, when she observed that the fallen
man again moved.   Rising on his hands and knees, he
crept forward a few paces, and then stopped.   Suddenly,
by a great effort, he raised himself to a kneeling position,
clasped his hands, and looked up.

The act sufficed to decide the wavering girl. Leaping lightly over the breastwork, she ran swiftly down until she reached the man, who gazed at her in open-mouthed astonishment. He was a white man, and the ghastly pallor of his face, with a few spots of blood on it and on his hands, told that he had been severely wounded.

"Manitou seems to have sent an angel of light to me in my extremity," he gasped in the Indian tongue.

"Com ; me vill help you," answered Softswan, in her broken English, as she stooped and assisted him to rise.

No other word was uttered, for even with the girl's assistance it was with the utmost difficulty that the man reached the breastwork of the hut, and when he had succeeded in clambering over it, he lay down and fainted.

After Softswan had glanced anxiously in the direction of the forest, and placed one of the guns in a handy position, she proceeded to examine the wounded stranger. Being expert in such matters, she opened his vest, and quickly found a wound near the region of the heart. It was bleeding steadily though not profusely. To stanch this and bind it up was the work of a few minutes. Then she reclosed the vest. In doing so she found something hard in a pocket near the wound. It was a little book, which she gently removed as it might interfere with the bandage. In doing so she

F

observed that the book had been struck by the bullet, which it deflected, so as to cause a more deadly wound than might otherwise have been inflicted.

She was thus engaged when the patient recovered consciousness, and, seizing her wrist, exclaimed, "Take not the Word from me. It has been my joy and comfort in all my—— "

He stopped on observing who it was that touched his treasure.

"Nay, then," he continued, with a faint smile, as he released his hold ; " it can come to no harm in thy keeping, child. For an instant I thought that rougher hands had seized it. But why remove it ?"

Softswan explained, but, seeing how eager the man was to keep it, she at once returned the little Bible to the inner pocket in which it was carried when not in use. Then running into the hut, she quickly returned with a rib of venison and a tin mug of water.

The man declined the food, but drained the mug with an air of satisfaction, which showed how much he stood in need of water.

Much refreshed, he pulled out the Bible again, and looked earnestly at it.

"Strange," he said, in the Indian tongue, turning his eyes on his surgeon-nurse ; " often have I heard of men saved from death by bullets being stopped by Bibles, but in my case it would seem as if God had made it a key to unlock the gates of the better land."

"Does my white father think he is going to die?" asked the girl in her own tongue, with a look of anxiety.

"It may be so," replied the man gently, "for I feel very, *very* weak. But feelings are deceptive; one cannot trust them. It matters little, however. If I live, it is to work for Jesus. If I die, it is to be with Jesus. But tell me, little one, who art thou whom the Lord has sent to succour me?"

"Me is Softswan, daughter of the great chief Bounding Bull," replied the girl, with a look of pride when she mentioned her father, which drew a slight smile from the stranger.

"But Softswan has white blood in her veins," he said; "and why does she sometimes speak in the language of the pale-face?"

"My mother," returned the girl in a low, sad tone, "was pale-face womans from the Saskatchewan. Me speaks Unglish, for my husban' likes it."

"Your husband—what is his name?"

"Big Tim."

"What!" exclaimed the wounded man with sudden energy, as a flush overspread his pale face; "is he the son of Little Tim, the brother-in-law of Whitewing the prairie chief?"

" He is the son of Leetil Tim, an' this be hims house."

"Then," exclaimed the stranger, with a pleased look, " I have reached, if not the end of my journey, at least a most important point in it, for I had appointed to meet Whitewing at this very spot, and did not know, when the Blackfoot Indian shot me, that I was so near the hut. It looked like a mere accident my finding the track which leads to it near the spot where I fell, but it is the Lord's doing. Tell me, Softswan, have you never heard White-wing and Little Tim speak of the pale-face missionary—the Preacher, they used to call me ?"

" Yes, yes, oftin," answered the girl eagerly. " Me tinks it bees you. Me *very* glad, an' Leetil Tim he——"

Her speech was cut short at this point by a repetition of the appalling war-whoop which had already disturbed the echoes of the gorge more than once that day.

Naturally the attention of Softswan had been some-what distracted by the foregoing conversation, and she had allowed the Indians to burst from the thicket and rush up the track a few paces before she was able to bring the big-bore gun to bear on them.

" Slay them not, Softswan," cried the preacher anxiously, as he tried to rise and prevent her firing. " We cannot escape them."

He was too late. She had already pressed the trigger, and the roar of the huge gun was reverberating from cliff to cliff like miniature thunder; but his cry had not been too late to produce wavering in the girl's mind, inducing her to take bad aim, so that the handful of slugs with which the piece had been charged went hissing over the assailants' heads instead of killing them. The stupendous hissing and noise, however, had the effect of momentarily arresting the savages, and inducing each man to seek the shelter of the nearest shrub.

"Com queek," cried Softswan, seizing the preacher's hand. "You be deaded soon if you not com queek."

Feeling the full force of this remark, the wounded man, exerting all his strength, arose, and suffered himself to be led into the hut. Passing quickly out by a door at the back, the preacher and the bride found themselves on a narrow ledge of rock, from one side of which was the precipice down which Big Tim had made his perilous descent. Close to their feet lay a great flat rock or natural slab, two yards beyond which the ledge terminated in a sheer precipice.

"No escape here," remarked the preacher sadly, as he looked round. "In my present state I could not venture down such a path even to save my life. But care not for me, Softswan. If you think you can escape, go and—— ".

He stopped, for to his amazement the girl stooped, and with apparent ease raised the ponderous mass of rock above referred to as though it had been a slight wooden trap-door, and disclosed a hole large enough for a man to pass through. The preacher observed that the stone was hinged on a strong iron bar, which was fixed considerably nearer to one side of it than the other. Still, this hinge did not account for the ease with which a mere girl lifted a ponderous mass which two or three men could not have moved without the aid of levers.

But there was no time to investigate the mystery of the matter, for another ringing war-whoop told that the Blackfeet, having recovered from their consternation, had summoned courage to renew the assault.

"Down queek!" said the girl, looking earnestly into her companion's face, and pointing to the dark hole, where the head of a rude ladder, dimly visible, showed what had to be done.

"It does not require much faith to trust and obey such a leader," thought the preacher, as he got upon the ladder, and quickly disappeared in the hole. Softswan lightly followed. As her head was about to disappear, she raised her hand, seized hold of a rough projection on the under surface of the mass of rock, and drew it gently down so as to effectually close the hole, leaving no trace whatever of its existence.

While this was going on the Blackfeet were advancing up the narrow pathway with superlative though needless caution, and no small amount of timidity. Each man

"DOWN QUEEK!" SAID THE GIRL.—Page 86.

took advantage of every scrap of cover he could find on the way up, but as the owner of the hut had taken care to remove all cover that was removable, they did not find much, and if the defenders had been there, that little would have been found to be painfully insufficient, for it consisted only of rugged masses and projections of rock, none of which could altogether conceal the figure of a full-grown man. Indeed, it seemed inexplicable that these Indians should have made this assault in broad day, considering that Indians in general are noted for their care of "number one," are particularly unwilling to meet their foes in fair open fight, and seldom if ever venture to storm a place of strength except by surprise and under the cover of night.

The explanation lay partly in the fact that they were aware of the advance of friends towards the place, but much more in this, that the party was led by the great chief Rushing River, a man possessed of that daring bulldog courage and reckless contempt of death which is usually more characteristic of white than of red men.

When the band had by galvanic darts and rushes gained the last scrap of cover that lay between them and the little fortress, Rushing River gave vent to a whoop which was meant to thrill the defenders with consternation to the very centre of their being, and made a gallant rush, worthy of his name, for the breastwork. Reaching it in gasping haste, he and his braves crouched for one moment at the foot of it, presumably to recover wind and allow the first fire of the defenders to pass over their heads.

But no first fire came, and Rushing River rolled his great black eyes upward in astonishment, perhaps thinking that his whoop had thrilled the defenders off the face of the earth altogether!

Suspense, they say, is less endurable than actual collision with danger. Probably Rushing River thought it so, for next moment he raised his black head quickly. Finding a hole in the defences, he applied one of his black eyes to it and peeped through. Seeing nothing, he uttered another whoop, and vaulted over like a squirrel, tomahawk in hand, ready to brain anybody or anything. Seeing nobody and nothing in particular, except an open door, he suspected an ambush in that quarter, darted round the corner of the hut to get out of the doorway line of fire, and peeped back.

Animated by a similar spirit, his men followed suit. When it became evident that no one meant to come out of the hut, Rushing River resolved to go in, and did so with another yell and a flourish of his deadly weapon, but again was he doomed to expend his courage and violence on air, for he possessed too much of natural dignity to expend his wrath on inanimate furniture.

Of course one glance sufficed to show that the defenders had flown, and it needed not the practised wit of a savage to perceive that they had retreated through the back door. In his eagerness to catch the foe, the Indian chief sprang after them with such a rush that nothing but a stout willow, which he grasped convulsively, prevented him from going over the precipice headlong—changing, as it were, from a River into a Fall—and ending his career appropriately in the torrent below.

When the chief had assembled his followers on the limited surface of the ledge, they all gazed around them for a few seconds in silence. On one side was a sheer precipice. On another side was, if we may so express it, a sheerer precipice rising upward. On the third side was the steep and rugged path, which looked sufficiently dangerous to arrest all save the mad or the desperate. On the fourth side was the hut.

Seeing all this at a glance, Rushing River looked mysterious and said, " Ho !"

To which his men returned, " How !" " Hi !" and "Hee !" or some other exclamation indicative of bafflement and surprise.

Standing on the trap-door rock as on a sort of pulpit, the chief pointed with his finger to the precipitous path, and said solemnly—

" Big Tim has gone down *there*. He has not the wings

of the hawk, but he has the spirit of the squirrel, or the legs of the goat."

" Or the brains of the fool," suggested a follower, with a few drops of white blood in his veins, which made him what boys call " cheeky."

" Of course," continued Rushing River, still more solemnly, and scorning to notice the remark, " of course Rushing River and his braves could follow if they chose. They could do anything. But of what use would it be? As well might we follow the moose-deer when it has got a long start."

" Big Tim has got the start, as Rushing River wisely says," remarked the cheeky comrade, " but he is hampered with his squaw, and cannot go fast."

" Many pale-faces are hampered by their squaws, and cannot go fast," retorted the chief, by which reply he meant to insinuate that the few drops of white blood in the veins of the cheeky one might yet come through an experience to which a pure Indian would scorn to submit. " But," continued the chief, after a pause to let the stab take full effect, " but Softswan is well known. She is strong as the mountain sheep and fleet as the mustang. She will not hamper Big Tim. Enough! We will let them go, and take possession of their goods."

Whatever the chief's followers might have thought about the first part of his speech, there was evidently no difference of opinion as to the latter part. With a series of assenting "Ho's," "How's," "Hi's," and "Hee's," they returned with him into the hut, and began to appropriate the property, commencing with a cold haunch of venison which they discovered in the larder, and to which they did ample justice, sitting in a circle on the floor in the middle of the little room.

Leaving them there, we will return to Softswan and her new friend.

"The place is very dark," remarked the preacher, groping cautiously about after the trap-door was closed as above described.

"Stan' still; I vill strik light," said Softswan.

In a few moments sparks were seen flying from flint and steel, and after one or two unsuccessful efforts a piece of tinder was kindled. Then the girl's pretty little nose and lips were seen of a fiery red colour as she blew some dry grass and chips into a flame, and kindled a torch therewith.

The light revealed a small natural cavern of rock, not much more than six feet high and ten or twelve wide, but of irregular shape, and extending into obscurity in one direction. The only objects in the cave besides the ladder by which they entered it were a few barrels partially covered with deerskin, an unusually small table, rudely but strongly made, and an enormous mass of rock enclosed in a net of strong rope which hung from an iron hook in the roof.

The last object at once revealed the mystery of the trap-door. It formed a ponderous counterpoise attached to the smaller section of the stone slab, and so nearly equalised the weight on the hinge that, as we have seen, Softswan's weak arm was sufficient to turn the scale.

The instant the torch flared up the girl stuck it into a crevice in the wall, and quickly grasping the little table, pushed it under the pendent rock. It reached to within half an inch of the mass. Picking up two broad wooden wedges that lay on the floor, she thrust them between the rock and the table, one on either side, so as to cause it to rest entirely on the table, and thus by removing its weight from the iron hook, the slab was rendered nearly immovable. She was anxiously active in these various operations, for already the Indians had entered the hut, and their voices could be distinctly heard overhead.

"Now," she whispered, with a sigh of relief, "six mans not abil to move the stone, even if he knowed the hole is b'low it."

"It is an ingenious device," said the preacher, throwing his exhausted form on a heap of pine branches which lay in a corner. "Who invented it—your husband?"

"No; it was Leetil Tim," returned the girl, with a low musical laugh. "Big Tim says hims fadder be great at 'ventions. He 'vent many t'ings. Some's good, some's bad, an' some's funny."

The preacher could not forbear smiling at this account of his old friend, in spite of his anxiety lest the Indians who were regaling themselves overhead should discover their retreat. He had begun to put some questions to Softswan in a low voice when he was rendered dumb and his blood seemed to curdle as he heard stumbling footsteps approaching from the dark end of the cavern. Then was heard the sound of some one panting vehemently. Next moment a man leaped into the circle of light, and seized the Indian girl in his arms.

"Thank God!" he exclaimed fervently; "not too late! I had thought the reptiles had been too much for thee, soft one. Ah me! I fear that some poor pale-face has——" He stopped abruptly, for at that moment Big Tim's eye fell upon the wounded man. "What!" he exclaimed, hastening to the preacher's side; "you *have* got here after all?"

"Ay, young man, through the goodness of God I have reached this haven of rest. Your words seem to imply that you had half expected to find me, though how you came to know of my case at all is to me a mystery."

"My white father," returned Big Tim, referring as much to the preacher's age and pure white hair as to his connection with the white men, "finds mystery where the hunter and the red man see none. I went out a-purpose to see that it was not my daddy the Blackfoot reptiles had shot, and soon came across your tracks, which showed me as plain as a book that you was badly wounded. I followed the tracks for a bit, expectin' to find you lyin' dead somewheres, when the whoops of the reptiles turned me back. But tell me, white father, are you not the preacher that my daddy and Whitewing used to know some twenty years agone?"

"I am, and fain would I meet with my former friends once more before I die."

"You shall meet with them, I doubt not," replied the young hunter, arranging the couch of the wounded man more comfortably. "I see that my soft one has bandaged you up, and she's better than the best o' sawbones at such work. I'll be able to make you more comfortable when we drive the reptiles out o'—— "

"Call them not reptiles," interrupted the preacher gently. "They are the creatures of God, like ourselves."

"It may be so, white father; nevertheless, they are uncommon low, mean, sneakin', savage critters, an' that's all that I've got to do with."

"You say truth, Big Tim," returned the preacher, "and that is also all that I have got to do with; but you and I take different methods of correcting the evil."

"Every man must walk in the ways to which he was

nat'rally born," rejoined the young hunter, with a dark frown, as the sound of revelry in the hut overhead became at the moment much louder; "my way wi' them may not be the best in the world, but you shall see in a few minutes that it is a way which will cause the very marrow of the rep—of the *dear* critters—to frizzle in their bones."

CHAPTER VII.

BIG TIM'S METHOD WITH SAVAGES.

"I SINCERELY hope," said the wounded man, with a look of anxiety, "that the plan you speak of does not involve the slaughter of these men."

"It does not," replied Big Tim, "though if it did, it would be serving them right, for they would slaughter you and me—ay, and even Softswan there—if they could lay hold of us."

"Is it too much to ask the son of my old friend to let me know what his plans are? A knowledge of them would perhaps remove my anxiety, which I feel pressing heavily on me in my present weak condition. Besides, I may be able to counsel you. Although a man of peace, my life has been but too frequently mixed up with scenes of war and bloodshed. In truth, my mission on earth is to teach those principles which, if universally acted on, would put an end to both;—perhaps I should have said, my mission is to point men to that Saviour who is an embodiment of the principles of Love and Peace and Goodwill."

For a few seconds the young hunter sat on the floor of the cave in silence, with his hands clasped round his knees, and his eyes cast down as if in meditation. At last a smile played on his features, and he looked at his questioner with a humorous twinkle in his eyes.

"Well, my white father," he said, " I see no reason why I should not explain the matter to my daddy's old friend; but I 'll have to say my say smartly, for by the stamping and yells o' the rep—o' the Blackfeet overhead, I perceive that they 've got hold o' my case-bottle o' rum, an' if I don't stop them they 'll pull the old hut down about their ears.

"Well, you must know that my daddy left the settlements in his young days," continued Big Tim, " an' took to a rovin' life on the prairies an' mountains, but p'r'aps he told you that long ago. No? Well, he served for some time at a queer sort o' trade—the makin' o' fireworks; them rediklous things they call squibs, crackers, rockets, an' Roman candles, with which the foolish folk o' the settlements blow their money into smoke for the sake o' ticklin' their fancies for a few minutes.

"Well, when he came here, of course he had no use for sitch tomfooleries, but once or twice, when he wanted to astonish the natives, he got hold o' some 'pothicary's stuff, an' wi' gunpowder an' charcoal concocted some things that wellnigh drove the red men out o' their senses, an' got daddy to be regarded as a great medicine-man. Of course he kep' it secret how he produced the surprisin' fires— an', to say truth, I think from my own experience that if he had tried to explain it to 'em they could have made neither head nor tail o't. For a long time arter that he did nothin' more in that way, till one time when the Blackfeet came an' catched daddy an' me nappin' in this very hut, and we barely got off wi' the scalps on our heads by scrambling down the precipice where the reptiles didn't like to follow. When they left the place they took all our odds an' ends wi' them, an' set fire to the hut. Arter they was gone we set to work an' built a noo hut. Then daddy—who's got an amazin' turn for inventin' things—set to work to concoct suthin' for the reptiles if they should pay us another visit. It was at that time he thought of turnin' this cave to account as a place o' refuge when hard pressed, an' hit on the plan for liftin' the big stone easy, which no doubt you 've obsarved."

"Yes; Softswan has explained it to me. But what about your plan with the Indians?" said the preacher.

"I'm comin' to that," replied the hunter. "Well, daddy set to work an' made a lot o' fireworks—big squibs, an' them sort o' crackers, I forget what you call 'em, that jumps about as if they was not only alive, but possessed with evil spirits—— "

"I know them—zigzag crackers," said the preacher, somewhat amused.

"That's them," cried Big Tim, with an eager look, as if the mere memory of them were exciting. "Well, daddy he fixed up a lot o' the big squibs an' Roman candles round the walls o' the hut in such a way that they all p'inted from ivery corner, above an' below, to the centre of the hut, right in front o' the fireplace, so that their fire should all meet, so to speak, in a focus. Then he chiselled out a lot o' little holes in the stone walls in such a way that they could not be seen, and in every hole he put a zigzag cracker; an' he connected the whole affair— squibs, candles, and crackers—with an instantaneous fuse, the end of which he trained down, through a hole cut in the solid rock, into this here cave; an' there's the end of it right opposite to yer nose."

He pointed as he spoke to a part of the wall of the cavern where a small piece of what seemed like white tape projected about half an inch from the stone.

"Has it ever been tried?" asked the preacher, who, despite his weak and wounded condition, could hardly restrain a laugh as the young hunter described his father's complicated arrangements.

"No, we han't tried it yet, 'cause the reptiles haven't

bin here since, but daddy, who's a very thoroughgoin' man, has given the things a complete overhaul once a month ever since—'cept when he was away on long expeditions—so as to make sure the stuff was dry an' in workin' order.   Now," added the young man, rising and lighting a piece of tinder at the torch on the wall, "it's about time that we should putt it to the test.   If things don't go wrong, you'll hear summat koorious overhead before long."

He applied a light to the quick-match as he spoke, and awaited the result.

In order that the reader may observe that result more clearly, we will transport him to the scene of festivity in the little fortress above.

As Big Tim correctly surmised, the savages had discovered the hunter's store of rum just after eating as much venison as they could comfortably consume.   Firewater, as is well known, tells with tremendous effect on the excitable nerves and minds of Indians.   In a very few minutes it produced, as in many white men, a tendency to become garrulous.   While in this stage the savages began to boast, if possible, more than usual of their prowess in chase and war, and as their potations continued, they were guilty of that undignified act—so rare among red men and so common among whites—of interrupting and contradicting each other.

This condition is the sure precursor of the quarrelsome and fighting stage of drunkenness. They had almost reached it, when Rushing River rose to his feet for the purpose of making a speech. Usually the form of the chief was as firm as the rock on which he stood. At this time, however, it swayed very slightly to and fro, and in his eyes—which were usually noted for the intensity of their eagle glance—there was just then an owlish blink as they surveyed the circle of his braves.

Indeed Rushing River, as he stood there looking down into the upturned faces, observed—with what feelings we know not—that these braves sometimes exhibited a few of the same owlish blinks in their earnest eyes.

"My b—braves," said the chief; and then, evidently forgetting what he intended to say, he put on one of those looks of astonishing solemnity which fire-water alone is capable of producing.

"My b—braves," he began again, looking sternly round the almost breathless and expectant circle, " when we left our l—lodges in the m—mountains this morning the sun was rising."

He paused, and this being an emphatic truism, was received with an equally emphatic " Ho" of assent.

" N—now," continued the chief, with a gentle sway to the right, which he corrected with an abrupt jerk to the left, "n—now, the sun is about to descend, and w—we are *here !*"

Feeling that he had made a decided point, he drew himself up and blinked, while his audience gave vent to another "Ho" in tones which expressed the idea—"waiting for more." The comrade, however, whose veins were fired, or chilled, with the few drops of white blood, ventured to assert his independence by ejaculating "Hum!"

"Bounding Bull," cried the chief, suddenly shifting ground and glaring, while he breathed hard and showed his teeth, "is a coward. His daughter Softswan is a chicken-hearted squaw ; and her husband Big Tim is a skunk—so is Little Tim his father."

These remarks, being thoroughly in accord with the sentiments of the braves, were received with a storm of "Ho's," "How's," "Hi's," and "Hee's, "which effectually drowned the cheeky one's "Hum's," and greatly encouraged the chief, who thereafter broke forth in a flow of language which was more in keeping with his name. After a few boastful references to the deeds of himself and his forefathers, he went into an elaborate and exaggerated description of the valorous way in which they had that day stormed the fort of their pale-face enemies and driven them out; after which, losing somehow the thread of his discourse, he fell back on an appallingly solemn look, blinked, and sat down.

This was the signal for the recurrence of the approving "Ho's" and "Hi's," the gratifying effect of which, however, was slightly marred when silence was restored by a subdued " Hum " from the cheeky comrade.

Directing a fierce glance at that presumptuous brave, Rushing River was about to give vent to words which might have led on to the fighting stage, when he was arrested, and, with his men, almost petrified, by a strange fizzing noise which seemed to come from the earth directly below them.

Incomprehensible sounds are at all times more calculated to alarm than sounds which we recognise. The report of a rifle, the yell of a foe, could not have produced such an effect on the savages as did that fizzing sound. Each man grasped his tomahawk, but sat still, and turned pale. The fizzing sound was interspersed with one or two cracks, which intensified the alarm, but did not clear up the mystery. If they had only known what to do they would have done it; what danger to face, they would have faced it; but to sit there inactive, with the mysterious sounds increasing, was almost intolerable.

Rushing River, of all the band, maintained his character for reckless hardihood. He sat there unblenched and apparently unmoved, though it was plain that he was intensely watchful and ready. But the foe assailed him where least expected. In a little hole right under the very spot on which he sat lay one of the zigzag crackers. Its first crack caused the chief, despite his power of will and early training, to bound up as if an electric battery had discharged him. The second crack sent the eccentric thing into his face. Its third vagary brought it down about his knees. Its fourth sent it into the gaping mouth of the cheeky one. At the same instant the squibs and candles burst forth from all points, pouring their fires on the naked shoulders of the red men with a hiss that the whole serpent race of America might have failed to equal, while the other zigzags went careering about as if the hut were filled with evil spirits.

To say that the savages yelled and jumped, and stamped and roared, were but a tame remark. After a series of wild bursts, in sudden and violent confusion which words cannot describe, they rushed in a compact body to the door. Of course they stuck fast. Rushing River went at them like a battering-ram, and tried to force them through, but failed. The cheeky comrade, with a better appreciation of the possibilities of the case, took a short run and a header right over the struggling mass, *à la harlequin*, and came down on his shoulders outside, without breaking his neck.

Guessing the state of things by the nature of the sounds, Big Tim removed the table from under the ponderous weight, lifted the re-adjusted trap-door, and,

A FIERY TRIAL.—Page 106.

springing up, darted into the hut just in time to bestow a parting kick on the last man that struggled through. Running to the breastwork, he beheld his foes tumbling, rushing, crashing, bounding down the track like maniacs —which indeed they were for the time being—and he succeeded in urging them to even greater exertions by giving utterance to a grand resonant British cheer, which had been taught him by his father, and had indeed been used by him more than once, with signal success, against his Indian foes.

Returning to the cavern after the Indians had vanished into their native woods, Big Tim assisted the preacher up the ladder, and, taking him into the hut after the smoke of the fireworks had cleared away, placed him in his own bed.

" You resemble your father in face, Big Tim, but not in figure," said the missionary, when he had recovered from the exhaustion caused by his recent efforts and excitement.

"My white father says truth," replied the hunter, with slightly humorous glances at his huge limbs. " Daddy is little, but he is strong—uncommon strong."

"He used to be so when I knew him," returned the preacher, " and I dare say the twenty years that have passed since then have not changed him much, for he is a good deal younger than I am—about the same age, I should suppose, as my old friend Whitewing."

"Yes, that's so," said the hunter; "they're both about five-an'-forty or there-away, though I doubt if either o' them is quite sure about his age. An' they're both beginning to be grizzled about the scalp-locks."

"Your father, although somewhat reckless in his disposition," continued the preacher, after a pause, "was a man of earnest mind."

"That's a fact, an' no mistake," returned Big Tim, examining a pot of soup which his bride had put on the fire to warm up for their visitor. "I doubt if ever I saw a more arnest-minded man than daddy, especially when he tackles his victuals or gets on the track of a grizzly b'ar."

The missionary smiled, in spite of himself, as he explained that the earnestness he referred to was connected rather with the soul and the spiritual world than with this sublunary sphere.

"Well, he is arnest about that too," returned the hunter. "He has often told me that he didn't use to trouble his head about such matters long ago, but after that time when he met you on the prairies he had been led to think a deal more about 'em. He's a queer man is daddy, an' putts things to ye in a queer way sometimes. 'Timmy,' says he to me once—he calls me Timmy out o' fondness, you know—'Timmy,' says he, 'if you comed up to a great thick glass wall, not very easy to see through, wi' a door in it, an' you was told that some day that door would open, an' you'd have to go through an' live on the other side o' that glass wall, you'd be koorious to know the lie o' the land on the other side o' that wall, wouldn't you, and what sort o' customers you'd have to consort wi' there, eh?"

"'Yes, daddy,' says I, 'you say right, an' I'd be a great fool if I didn't take a good long squint now an' again.'

"'Well, Timmy,' says he, 'this world is that glass wall, an' death is the door through it, an' the Bible that the preacher gave me long ago is the Book that helps to clear up the glass an' enable us to see through it a little better; an' a Blackfoot bullet or arrow may open the door to you an' me any day, so I'd advise you, lad, to take a good squint now an' again.' An' I've done it, too, Preacher, I've done it, but there's a deal on it that I don't rightly understand."

"That I do not wonder at, my young friend; and I hope that if God spares me I may be able to help you a little in this matter. But what of Whitewing? Has he never tried to assist you?"

"Tried! He just has; but the chief is too deep for me most times. He seems to have a wonderful grip o' these things himself, an' many a long palaver he has wi' my daddy about 'em. Whitewing does little else, in fact, but go about among his people far an' near tellin' them about

their lost condition and the Saviour of sinners.   He has
even ventur'd to visit a tribe o' the Blackfeet, but his
great enemy Rushin' River has sworn to scalp him if he
gets hold of him, so we 've done our best to hold him
back—daddy an' me—for it would be of no use preachin'
to such a double-dyed villain as Rushin' River."

" That is one of the things," returned the preacher,
" that you do not quite understand, Big Tim, for it was to
such men as he that our Saviour came.   Indeed, I have
returned to this part of the country for the very purpose of
visiting the Blackfoot chief in company with Whitewing."

" Both you and Whitewing will be scalped if you do,"
said the young hunter almost sternly.

" I trust not," returned the preacher ; " and we hope to
induce your father to go with us."

" Then daddy will be scalped too," said Big Tim—" an'
so will I, for I 'm bound to keep daddy company."

" It is to be hoped your gloomy expectations will not
be realised," returned the preacher.   " But tell me, where
is your father just now ? "

" Out hunting, not far off," replied the youth, with an
anxious look.   " To say truth, I don't feel quite easy about
him, for he 's bin away longer than usual, or than there 's
any occasion for.   If he doesn't return soon, I 'll have to
go an' sarch for him."

As the hunter spoke the hooting of an owl was

distinctly heard outside. The preacher looked up inquiringly, for he was too well acquainted with the ways of Indians not to know that the cry was a signal from a biped without wings. He saw that Big Tim and his bride were both listening intently, with expressions of joyful expectation on their faces.

Again the cry was heard, much nearer than before.

"Whitewing!" exclaimed the hunter, leaping up and hastening to the door.

Softswan did not move, but continued silently to stir the soup in the pot on the fire.

Presently many footsteps were heard outside, and the sound of men conversing in low tones. Another moment, and a handsome middle-aged Indian stood in the doorway. With an expression of profound sorrow, he gazed for one moment at the wounded man; then, striding forward, knelt beside him and grasped his hand.

"My white father!" he said.

"Whitewing!" exclaimed the preacher; "I little expected that our meeting should be like this!"

"Is the preacher badly hurt?" asked the Indian in a low voice.

"It may be so; I cannot tell. My feelings lead me to—to doubt—I was going to say fear, but I have nothing to fear. 'He doeth all things well.' If my work on earth is not done, I shall live; if it is finished, I shall die."

CHAPTER VIII.

NETTING A GRIZZLY BEAR.

A S it is at all times unwise as well as disagreeable to involve a reader in needless mystery, we may as well explain here that there would have been no mystery at all in Little Tim's prolonged absence from his fortress, if it had not been that he was aware of the intended visit of his chum and brother-in-law, Whitewing, and his old friend the pale-faced missionary, and that he had promised to return on the evening of the day on which he set off to hunt, or on the following morning at latest.

Moreover, Little Tim was a man of his word, having never within the memory of his oldest friend been known to break it. Thus it came to pass that when three days had passed away, and the sturdy little hunter failed to return, Big Tim and his bride first became surprised and then anxious. The attack on the hut, however, and the events which we have just related, prevented the son from going out in search of the father; but now that the

Blackfeet had been effectually repulsed and the fortress relieved by the arrival of Whitewing's party, it was resolved that they should organise a search for the absentee without an hour's delay.

"Leetil Tim," said Whitewing decisively, when he was told of his old friend's unaccountable absence, " must be found."

" So say I," returned Big Tim. " I hope the Blackfoot reptiles haven't got him. Mayhap he has cut himself with his hatchet. Anyhow, we must go at once. You won't mind our leaving you for a bit ? " he added, turning to the missionary; " we will leave enough o' redskins to guard you, and my soft one will see to it that you are comfortable."

"Think not of me," replied the preacher. " All will go well, I feel assured."

Still further to guard the reader from supposing that there is any mystery connected with the missionary's name or Little Tim's surname, we think it well to state at once that there is absolutely none. In those outlandish regions, and among that primitive people, the forming of names by the mere combination of unmeaning syllables found small favour. They named people according to some striking quality or characteristic. Hence our missionary had been long known among the red men of the West as the Preacher, and, being quite satisfied with that name, he accepted it without making any attempt to bamboozle the children of the woods and prairies with his real name, which was—and is—a matter of no importance whatever. Tim likewise, being short of stature, though very much the reverse of weak or diminutive, had accepted the name of " Little Tim" with a good grace, and made mention of no other; his son naturally becoming " Big Tim" when he outgrew his father.

A search expedition having been quickly organised, it left the little fortress at once, and defiled into the thick woods, led by Whitewing and Big Tim.

In order that the reader may fully understand the cause of Little Tim's absence, we will take the liberty of pushing on in advance of the search party, and explain a few matters as we go.

It has already been shown that our little hunter possessed a natural ingenuity of mind. This quality had, indeed, been noticeable when he was a boy, but it did not develop largely till he became a man. As he grew older his natural ingenuity seemed to become increasingly active, until his thirst for improving on mechanical contrivances and devising something new became almost a passion. Hence he was perpetually occupied in scheming to improve—as he was wont to say—the material condition of the human race, as well as the mental.

Among other things, he improved the traps of his

Indian friends, and also their dwellings. He invented new traps, and, as we have seen, new methods of defending dwellings, as well as of escaping when defence failed. His name, of course, became well known in the Indian country, and as some of his contrivances proved to be eminently useful, he was regarded far and near as a great medicine-man, who could do whatever he set his mind to. Without laying claim to such unlimited powers, Little Tim was quite content to leave the question of his capacity to scheme and invent as much a matter of uncertainty in the minds of his red friends as it was in his own mind.

One day there came to the Indian village, in which he dwelt at the time with his still pretty though matronly wife Brighteyes, one of the agents of a man whose business it was to collect wild animals for the menageries of the United States and elsewhere. Probably this man was an ancestor of Barnum, for he possessed a mind which seemed to be capable of conceiving anything and sticking at nothing. He found a man quite after his own heart when he discovered Little Tim.

"I want a grizzly b'ar," he said, on being introduced to the hunter.

"There's plenty of 'em in these parts," said Tim, who was whittling a piece of wood at the time.

"But I want a full-grown old 'un," said the agent.

"Well," remarked Tim, looking up with an inquiring

glance for a moment, "I should say there's some thousands, more or less, roamin' about the Rockies, in all stages of oldness—from experienced mammas to great-grand-mothers, to say nothin' o' the old gentlemen; but you'll find most of 'em powerful sly an' uncommon hard to kill."

"But I don't want to kill 'em; I want one of 'em alive," said the agent.

At this little Tim stopped whittling the bit of stick, and looked hard at the man,

"You wants to catch one alive?" he repeated.

"Yes, that's what's the matter with me exactly. I want it for a show, an' I'm prepared to give a good price for a big one."

"How much?" asked the hunter.

The stranger bent down and whispered in his ear. Little Tim raised his eyebrows a little, and resumed whittling.

"But," said he, after a few moments' vigorous knife-work, "what if I should try, an' fail?"

"Then you get nothing."

"Won't do," returned the little hunter, with a slow shake of the head. "I'm game to tackle difficulties for love *or* money, but not for nothin'. You'll have to go to another shop, stranger.".

"Well, what will you *try* it for?" asked the agent, who was unwilling to lose his man.

"For quarter o' the sum down, to be kep' whether I succeed or fail, the balance to be paid when I hand over the goods."

"Well, stranger," returned the agent, with a grim smile, "I don't mind if I agree to that. You seem an honest man."

"Sorry I can't return the compliment," said Little Tim, holding out his hand. "So cash down, if you please."

The agent laughed, but pulled out a huge leathern bag, and paid the stipulated sum in good undeniable silver dollars.

The hunter at once made preparation for his enterprise. Meanwhile the agent took up his abode in the Indian village to await the result.

After a night of profound meditation in the solitude of his wigwam, Little Tim set to work and cut up several fresh buffalo hides into long and strong lines with which he made a net of enormous mesh and strength. He arranged it in such a way, with a line run round the circumference, that he could draw it together like a purse. With this gigantic affair on his shoulder, he set off one morning at daybreak into the mountains. He met the agent, who was an early riser, on the threshold of the village.

"What! goin' out alone, Little Tim?" he said.

"Yes; b'ars don't like company, as a rule."

" Don't you think I might help you a bit ? "

" No, I don't.   If you stop where you are, I 'll very likely bring the b'ar home to 'ee.   If you go with me, it 's more than likely the b'ar will take you home to her small family ! "

" Well, well, have it your own way," returned the agent, laughing.

" I a'ways do," replied the hunter, with a grin.

Proceeding a day's journey into the mountains, our adventurous hunter discovered the track of a bear, which must, he thought, be an uncommonly large one.   Selecting a convenient tree, he stuck four slender poles into the ground, under one of its largest branches.   Over these he spread his net, arranging the closing rope—or what we may term the purse-string—in such a way that he could pass it over the branch of the tree referred to.   This done, he placed a large junk of buffalo-meat directly under the net, and pegged it to the ground.

Thereafter Little Tim ascended the tree, crept out on the large limb until he reached the spot where the line had been thrown over it, directly above his net.   There, seating himself comfortably among the branches, he proceeded to sup and enjoy himself, despite the unsavoury smell that arose from the half-decayed buffalo-meat below.

The limb of the tree was so large and suitable that, while a fork of it was wide enough to serve for a table, a branch which grew upwards formed a lean to the hunter's back, and another branch, doubling round most conveniently, formed a rest for his right elbow. At the same time an abrupt curl in the same branch constituted a rest for his gun. Thus he reclined in a natural one-armed rustic chair, with his weapons handy, and a good supper before him.

"What could a man wish more?" he muttered to himself, with a contented expression of face, as he fixed a square piece of birch-bark in the fork of the branch, and on this platter arranged his food, commenting thereon as he proceeded : "Roast prairie hen. Capital grub, with a bit o' salt pork, though rather dry an' woodeny-like by itself. Buffalo rib. Nothin' better, hot or cold, except marrow-bones ; but then, you see, marrow-bones ain't just parfection unless hot, an' this is bound to be a cold supper. Hunk o' pemmican. A safe stand-by at all times. Don't need no cookin', an' a just proportion o' fat to lean, but doesn't do without appetite to make it go down. Let me be thankful I've got that, anyhow."

At this point Little Tim thought it expedient to make the line of his net fast to this limb of the tree. After doing so, he examined the priming of his gun, made a few other needful arrangements, and then gave himself up to the enjoyment of the hour, smiling benignly to the moon, which happened to creep out from behind a mountain peak at the time, as if on purpose to irradiate the scene.

"It has always seemed to me," muttered the hunter, as well as a large mouthful of the prairie hen would permit —for he was fond of muttering his thoughts when alone; it felt more sociable, you see, than merely thinking them—"It has always seemed to me that contentment is a grand thing for the human race. Pity we hasn't all got it!"

Inserting at this point a mass of the hunk, which proved a little too large for muttering purposes, he paused until the road was partially cleared, and then went on—

"Of course I don't mean that lazy sort o' contentment that makes a man feel easy an' comfortable, an' quite indifferent to the woes an' worries of other men so long as his own bread-basket is stuffed full. No, no. I means that sort o' contentment that makes a man feel happy though he hasn't got champagne an' taters, pigeon-pie, lopscouse, plum-duff, mustard an' jam at every blow-out; that sort o' contentment that takes things as they come, an' enjoys 'em without grumpin' an' growlin' 'cause he hasn't got somethin' else."

Another hunk here stopping the way, a somewhat longer silence ensued, which would probably have been broken as before by the outpouring of some sage reflections, but for a slight sound which caused the hunter to become what we may style a human petrifaction, with a half-chewed morsel in its open jaws, and its eyes glaring.

A few seconds more, and the sound of breaking twigs gave evidence that a visitor drew near. Little Tim bolted the unchewed morsel, hastily sheathed his hunting-knife, laid one hand on the end of his line, and waited.

He had not to wait long, for out of the woods there sauntered a grizzly bear of such proportions that the hunter at first thought the moonlight must have deceived him.

"Sartinly it's the biggest that I've ever clapped eyes on," he thought, but he did not speak or move. So anxious was he not to scare the animal, that he hardly breathed.

Bruin seemed to entertain suspicions of some sort, for he sniffed the tainted air once or twice, and looked inquiringly round. Coming to the conclusion, apparently, that his suspicions were groundless, he walked straight up to the lump of buffalo-meat and sniffed it. Not being particular, he tried it with his tongue.

"Good!" said the bear—at least if he did not say so, he must have thought so, for next moment he grasped it with his teeth. Finding it tethered hard and fast, he gathered himself together for the purpose of exercising main force.

Now was Little Tim's opportunity. Slipping a cord by which the net was suspended to the four stakes, he caused it to descend like a curtain over the bear. It acted most successfully, insomuch that the animal was completely enveloped.

Surprised, but obviously not alarmed, Bruin shook his head, sniffed a little, and pawed the part of the net in front of him. The hunter wasted no time. Seeing that the net was all right, he pulled with all his might on the main rope, which partly drew the circumference of the net together. Finding his feet slightly trammelled, the grizzly tried to move off, but of course trod on the net, tripped, and rolled over. In so doing he caught sight of the hunter, who was now enabled to close the mouth of the net-purse completely.

Being by that time convinced, apparently, that he was the victim of foul play, the bear lost his temper, and tried to rise. He tripped as before, came down heavily on his side, and hit the back of his head against a stone. This threw him into a violent rage, and he began to bounce.

At all times bouncing is ineffectual and silly, even in a grizzly bear. The only result was that he bruised his head and nose, tumbled among stones and stumps, and strained the rope so powerfully that the limb of the tree to which it was attached was violently shaken, and Little Tim was obliged to hold on to avoid being shaken off.

Experience teaches bears as well as fools. On discovering that it was useless to bounce, he sat down in a disconsolate manner, poked as much as he could of his nose through one of the meshes, and sniggered at Little Tim, who during these outbursts was naturally in a state of great excitement. Then the bear went to work leisurely to gnaw the mesh close to his mouth.

The hunter was not prepared for this. He had counted on the creature struggling with its net till it was in a state of complete exhaustion, when, by means of additional ropes, it could be so wound round and entangled in every limb as to be quite incapable of motion. In this condition it might be slung to a long pole and carried by a sufficient number of men to the small, but immensely strong, cage on wheels which the agent had brought with him.

Not only was there the danger of the bear breaking loose and escaping, or rendering it necessary that he should be shot, but there was another risk which Little Tim had failed at first to note. The scene on which he had decided to play out his little game was on the gentle slope of a hill, which terminated in a precipice of considerable height, and each time the bear struggled and rolled over in his network purse, he naturally gravitated towards the precipice, over which he was certain to go if the rope which held him to the tree should snap.

The hunter had just become thoroughly alive to this danger when, with a tremendous struggle, the bear burst two of the meshes in rear, and his hind-quarters were free.

Little Tim seized his gun, feeling that the crisis had come. He was loath to destroy the creature, and hesitated. Instead of backing out of his prison, as he might easily

have done, the bear made use of his free hind legs to make
a magnificent bound forward.   He was checked, of course,
by the rope, but Tim had miscalculated the strength of
his materials.   A much stronger rope would have broken
under the tremendous strain.   The line parted like a
piece of twine, and the bear, rolling head over heels
down the slope, bounded over the precipice, and went
hurling out into space like a mighty football !

There was silence for a few seconds, then a simultaneous
thud and bursting cry that was eminently suggestive.

"H'm !   It's all over," sighed Little Tim, as he slid
down the branch to the ground.

And so it was.   The bear was effectually killed, and
the poor hunter had to return to the Indian village crestfallen.

"But hold on, stranger," he said, on meeting the agent;
"don't you give way to despair.   I said there was lots of
'em in these parts.   You come with me up to a hut my
son's got in the mountains, an' I'll circumvent a b'ar for
you yet.   You can't take the cart quite up to the hut, but
you can git near enough, at a place where there's a Injin'
friend o' mine as 'll take care of ye."

The agent agreed, and thus it came to pass that, at the
time of which we now write, Little Tim was doing his best
to catch a live bear, but, not liking to be laughed at even
by his son in the event of failure, he had led him and his

bride to suppose that he had merely gone out hunting in the usual way.

It was on this expedition that Little Tim had set forth when Whitewing was expected to arrive at Tim's Folly—as the little hut or fortress had come to be named—and it was the anxiety of his friends and kindred at his prolonged absence which resulted, as we have seen, in the formation and departure of a search expedition.

CHAPTER IX.

A DARING EXPLOIT.

TO practised woodsmen like Whitewing and Big Tim
it was as easy to follow the track of Little Tim as
if his steps had been taken through newly-fallen snow,
although very few and slight were the marks left on the
green moss and rugged ground over which the hunter had
passed.

Six picked Indians accompanied the prairie chief, and
these marched in single file, each treading in the footsteps
of the man in front with the utmost care.

At first the party maintained absolute silence. Their
way lay for some distance along the margin of the brawling stream which drained the gorge at the entrance of
which Tim's Folly stood. The scenery around them was
wild and savage in the extreme, for the higher they
ascended, the narrower became the gorge, and the masses
of rock which had fallen from the frowning cliffs on either
side had strewn the lower ground with shapeless blocks,

and so impeded the natural flow of the little stream that it became, as it were, a tormented and foaming cataract.

At the head of the gorge the party came to a pass or height of land, through which they went with caution, for, although no footsteps of man had thus far been detected by their keen eyes save those of Little Tim, it was not beyond the bounds of possibility that foes might be lurking on the other side of the pass. No one, however, was discovered, and when they emerged at the other end of the pass it was plain that, as Big Tim remarked, the coast was clear, for from their commanding position they could see an immeasurable distance in front of them, over an un-encumbered stretch of land.

The view from this point was indeed stupendous. The vision seemed to range not only over an almost limitless world of forests, lakes, and rivers—away to where the haze of the horizon seemed to melt with them into space —but beyond that to where the great backbone of the New World rose sharp, clear, and gigantic above the mists of earth, until they reached and mingled with the fleecy clouds of heaven. To judge from their glittering eyes, even the souls of the not very demonstrative Indians were touched by the scene. As for the prairie chief, who had risen to the perceptions of the new life in Christ, he halted and stood for some moments as if lost in con-

I

templation.   Then, turning to the young hunter at his side, he said softly—

"The works of the Lord are great."

"Strange," returned Big Tim, "that you should use the very same words that I 've heard my daddy use sometimes when we 've come upon a grand view like that."

"Not so strange when I tell you," replied Whitewing, "that these are words from the Book of Manitou, and that your father and I learned them together long ago from the preacher who now lies wounded in your hut."

"Ay, ay ! Daddy didn't tell me that.   He 's not half so given to serious talk as you are, Whitewing, though I 'm free to admit that he does take a fit o' that sort now an' again, and seems raither fond of it.   The fact is, I don't quite understand daddy.   He puzzles me."

"Perhaps Leetil Tim is too much given to fun when he talks with Big Tim," suggested the red chief gravely, but with a slight twinkle in his eyes, which told that he was not quite destitute of Little Tim's weakness—or strength, as the reader chooses.

After a brief halt, the party descended the slope which led to the elevated valley they had now reached, and, having proceeded a few miles, again came to a halt because the ground had become so rocky that the trail of the hunter was lost.

Ordering the young men to spread themselves over the

ground, Whitewing went with Big Tim to search over the ridge of a neighbouring eminence.

"It is as I expected," he said, coming to a sudden stand, and pointing to a faint mark on the turf. "Leetil Tim has taken the short cut to the Lopstick Hill, but I cannot guess the reason why."

Big Tim was down on his knees examining the footprints attentively.

"Daddy's futt, an' no mistake," he said, rising slowly. "I'd know the print of his heel among a thousand. He's got a sort o' swagger of his own, an' puts it down with a crash, as if he wanted to leave his mark wherever he goes. I've often tried to cure him o' that, but he's incurable."

"I have observed," returned the chief, with, if possible, increased gravity, "that many sons are fond of trying to cure their fathers; also, that they never succeed."

Big Tim looked quickly at his companion, and laughed.

"Well, well," he said, "the daddies have a good go at us in youth. It's but fair that we should have a turn at *them* afterwards."

A sharp signal from one of the young Indians in the distance interrupted further converse, and drew them away to see what he had discovered. It was obvious enough —the trail of the Blackfoot Indians retiring into the mountains.

At first Big Tim's heart sank, for this discovery, coupled

with the prolonged absence of his father, suggested the fear that he had been waylaid and murdered. But a further examination led them to think—at least to hope—that the savages had not observed the hunter's trail, owing to his having diverged at a point of the track further down, where the stony nature of the ground rendered trail-finding, as we have seen, rather difficult. Still, there was enough to fill the breasts of both son and friend with anxiety, and to induce them to push on thereafter swiftly and in silence.

Let us once again take flight ahead of them, and see what the object of their anxiety is doing.

True to his promise to try his best, the dauntless little hunter had proceeded alone, as before, to a part of the mountain region where he knew from past experience that grizzlies were to be easily found. There he made his preparations for a new effort on a different plan.

The spot he selected for his enterprise was an open space on a bleak hillside, where the trees were scattered and comparatively small. This latter peculiarity—the smallness of the trees—was, indeed, the only drawback to the place, for few of them were large enough to bear his weight, and afford him a secure protection from his formidable game. At last, however, he found one,—not, indeed, quite to his mind, but sufficiently large to enable him to get well out of a bear's reach, for it must be remembered that although some bears climb trees easily, the grizzly bear cannot climb at all. There was a branch on the lower part of the tree which seemed quite beyond the reach of the tallest bear even on tiptoe.

Having made his disposition very much as on the former occasion, Little Tim settled himself on this branch, and awaited the result.

He did not, however, sit as comfortably as on the previous occasion, for the branch was small and had no fork. Neither did he proceed to sup as formerly, for it was yet too early in the day to indulge in that meal.

His plan this time was, not to net, but to lasso the bear ; and for that purpose he had provided four powerful ropes made of strips of raw, undressed buffalo hide, plaited, with a running noose on each.

"Now," said Little Tim, with a self-satisfied smirk, as he seated himself on the branch and surveyed the four ropes complacently, "it'll puzzle the biggest b'ar in all the Rocky Mountains to break them ropes."

Any one acquainted with the strength of the material which Tim began to uncoil would have at once perceived that the lines in question might have held an elephant or a small steamer.

"I hope," murmured Tim, struggling with a knot in one of the cords that bound the coils, "I hope I'll be in luck to-day, an' won't have to wait long."

Little Tim's hope reached fruition sooner than he had expected—sooner even than he desired—for as he spoke he heard a rustle in the bushes behind him. Looking round quickly, he beheld "the biggest b'ar, out o' sight, that he had iver seen in all his life." So great was his surprise—we would not for a moment call it alarm—that he let slip the four coils of rope, which fell to the ground.

Grizzly bears, it must be known, are gifted with insatiable curiosity, and they are not troubled much with the fear of man, or, indeed, of anything else. Hearing the thud of the coils on the ground, this monster grizzly walked up to and smelt them. He was proceeding to taste them, when, happening to cast his little eyes upwards, he beheld Little Tim sitting within a few feet of his head. To rise on his hind legs, and solicit a nearer interview, was the work of a moment. To the poor hunter's alarm, when he stretched his tremendous paws and claws to their utmost he reached to within a foot of the branch. Of course Little Tim knew that he was safe, but he was obliged to draw up his legs and lay out on the branch, which brought his head and eyes horribly near to the nose and projecting tongue of the monster.

To make matters worse, Tim had left his gun leaning against the stem of the tree. He had his knife and hatchet in his belt, but these he knew too well were but feeble weapons against such a foe. Besides, his object was not to slay, but to secure.

Seeing that there was no possibility of reaching the hunter by means of mere length of limb, and not at that time having acquired the art of building a stone pedestal for elevating purposes, the bear dropped on its four legs and looked round. Perceiving the gun, it went leisurely up and examined it. The examination was brief but effective. It gave the gun only one touch with its paw, but that touch broke the lock and stock and bent the barrel so as to render the weapon useless.

Then it returned to the coil of ropes, and, sitting down, began to chew one of them, keeping a serious eye, however, on the branch above.

It was a perplexing situation even for a backwoodsman. The branch on which Tim lay was comfortable enough, having many smaller branches and twigs extending from it on either side, so that he did not require to hold on very tightly to maintain his position. But he was fully aware of the endurance and patience of grizzly bears, and knew that, having nothing else to do, this particular Bruin could afford to bide his time.

And now the ruling characteristic of Little Tim beset him severely. His head felt like a bombshell of fermenting ingenuity. Every device, mechanical and otherwise, that had ever passed through his brain since childhood, seemed to rush back upon him with irresistible violence in his hopeless effort to conceive some plan by which to escape from his present and pressing difficulty—he would not,. even to himself, admit that there was danger. The more hopeless the case appeared to him, the less did reason and common-sense preside over the fermentation. When he saw his gun broken, his first anxiety began. When he reflected on the persistency of grizzlies in watching their foes, his naturally buoyant spirits began to sink and his native recklessness to abate. When he saw the bear begin steadily to devour one of the lines by which he had hoped to capture it, his hopes declined still more ; and when he considered the distance he was from his hut, the fact that his provision wallet had been left on the ground along with the gun, and that the branch on which he rested was singularly unfit for a resting-place on which to pass many hours, he became wildly ingenious, and planned to escape, not only by pitching his cap to some distance off, so as to distract the bear's attention, and enable him to slip down and run away, but by devising methods of effecting his object by clockwork, fireworks, wings, balloons—in short, by everything that ever has, in the history of design, enabled men to achieve their ends.

His first and simplest method, to fling his cap away, was indeed so far successful that it did distract the bear's attention for a moment, but it did not disturb his huge body, for he sat still, chewing his buffalo quid leisurely, and, after a few seconds, looked up at his victim as though to ask, "What d' you mean by that?"

When, after several hours, all his attempts had failed, poor Little Tim groaned in spirit, and began to regret his having undertaken the job; but a sense of the humorous, even in that extremity, caused him to give vent to a short laugh as he observed that Bruin had managed to get several feet of the indigestible rope down his throat, and fancied what a surprise it would give him if he were to get hold of the other end of the rope and pull it all out again.

At last night descended on the scene, making the situation much more unpleasant, for the darkness tended to deceive the man as to the motions of the brute, and once or twice he almost leaped off the branch under the impression that his foe had somehow grown tall enough to reach him, and was on the point of seizing him with his formidable claws. To add to his troubles, hunger came upon Tim about his usual supper-time, and what was far worse, because much less endurable, sleep put in a powerful claim to attention. Indeed this latter difficulty became so great that hunger, after a time, ceased to trouble him, and all his faculties—even the inventive—were engaged in a tremendous battle with this good old friend, who had so suddenly been converted into an implacable foe. More than once that night did Little Tim, despite his utmost efforts, fall into a momentary sleep, from which each time he awoke with a convulsive start and sharp cry, to the obvious surprise of Bruin, who, being awakened out of a comfortable nap, looked up with a growl inquiringly, and then relapsed.

When morning broke, it found the wretched man still clutching his uneasy couch, and blinking like an owl at the bear, which still lay comfortably on the ground below him. Unable to stand it any longer, Tim resolved to have a short nap, even if it should cost him his life. With this end in view, he twined his arms and legs tightly round his branch. The very act reminded him that his worsted waist-belt might be twined round both body and branch, for it was full two yards long. Wondering that it had not occurred to him before, he hastily undid it, lashed himself to the branch as well as he could, and in a moment was sound asleep. This device would have succeeded admirably had not one of his legs slowly dropped so low down as to attract the notice of the bear when it awoke. Rising to its full height on its hind legs, and protruding its tongue to the utmost, it just managed to touch Tim's toe. The touch acted liked an electric spark, awoke him at once, and the leg was drawn promptly up.

But Tim had had a nap, and it is wonderful how brief a slumber will suffice to restore the energies of a man in robust health. He unlashed himself.

"Good mornin' to 'ee," he said, looking down. "You're there yet, I see."

He finished the salutation with a loud yawn, and stretched himself so recklessly that he almost fell off the branch into the embrace of his expectant foe. Then he looked round, and, reason having been restored, hit upon a plan of escape which seemed to him hopeful.

We have said that the space he had selected was rather open, but there were scattered over it several large masses of rock, about the size of an ordinary cart, which had fallen from the neighbouring cliffs. Four of these stood in a group at about fifty yards' distance from his tree.

"Now, old Caleb," he said, "I'll go in for it, neck or nothin'. You tasted my toes this mornin'. Would you like to try 'em again?"

He lowered his foot as he spoke, as far down as he could reach. The bear accepted the invitation at once, rose up, protruded his tongue as before, and just managed to touch the toe. Now it is scarcely needful to say that a strong man leading the life of a hunter in the Rocky Mountains is an athlete. Tim thought no more of swinging himself up into a tree by the muscular power of his arms than you would think of stepping over a narrow ditch. When the bear was standing in its most upright attitude, he suddenly swung down, held on to the branch with his hands, and drove both his feet with such force

against the bear's chin that it lost its balance and fell
over backwards with an angry growl. At the same
moment Tim dropped to the ground, and made for the
fallen rocks at a quicker rate than he had ever run before.
Bruin scrambled to his feet with amazing agility, looked
round, saw the fugitive, and gave chase. Darting past the
first rock, it turned, but Little Tim, of course, was not
there. He had doubled round the second, and taken
refuge behind the third mass of rock.

Waiting a moment till the baffled bear went to look
behind another rock, he ran straight back again to his tree,
hastily gathered up his ropes, and reascended to his branch,
where the bear found him again not many minutes later.

" Ha ! HA ! you old rascal ! " he shouted, as he fastened
the end of a rope firmly to the branch, and gathered in the
slack so as to have the running noose handy. " I've got
you now. Come, come along ; have another taste of my toe !"

This invitation was given when the bear stood in his
former position under the tree and looked up. Once
again it accepted the invitation, and rose to the hunter's
toe as a salmon rises to an irresistible fly.

" That's it ! Now, hold on—just one moment. *There !* "

As Tim finished the sentence, he dropped the noose so
deftly over the bear's head and paws that it went right
down to his waist. This was an unlooked-for piece of
good fortune. The utmost the hunter had hoped for was

to noose the creature round the neck. Moreover, it was done so quickly that the monster did not seem to fully appreciate what had occurred, but continued to strain and reach up at the toe in an imbecile sort of way. Instead, therefore, of drawing the noose tight, Little Tim dropped a second noose round the monster's neck, and drew that tight. Becoming suddenly alive to its condition, the grizzly made a backward plunge, which drew both ropes tight and nearly strangled it, while the branch on which Tim was perched shook so violently that it was all he could do to hold on.

For full half an hour that bear struggled fiercely to free itself, and often did the shaken hunter fear that he had miscalculated the strength of his ropes, but they stood the test well, and, being elastic, acted in some degree like lines of indiarubber. At the end of that time the bear fell prone from exhaustion, which, to do him justice, was more the result of semi-strangulation than exertion.

This was what Little Tim had been waiting for and expecting. Quietly but quickly he descended to the ground, but the bear saw him, partially recovered, no doubt under an impulse of rage, and began to rear and plunge again, compelling his foe to run to the fallen rocks for shelter. When Bruin had exhausted himself a second time, Tim ran forward and seized the old net with which he had failed to catch the previous bear, and threw it over his captive. The act of course revived the lively monster, but his struggles now wound him up into such a ravel with the two lines and the net that he was soon unable to get up or jump about, though still able to make the very earth around him tremble with his convulsive heaves. It was at once a fine as well as an awful display of the power of brute force and the strength of raw material!

Little Tim would have admired it with philosophic interest if he had not been too busy dancing around the writhing creature in a vain effort to fix his third rope on a hind leg. At last an opportunity offered. A leg burst one of the meshes of the net. Tim deftly slipped the noose over it, and made the line fast to the tree. "Now," said he, wiping the perspiration from his brow, "you're safe, so I'll have a meal."

And Little Tim, sitting down on a stone at a respectful distance, applied himself with zest to the cold breakfast of which he stood so very much in need.

He was thus occupied when his son with the prairie chief and his party found him.

It would take at least another chapter to describe adequately the joy, surprise, laughter, gratulation, and comment which burst from the rescue party on discovering the hunter. We therefore leave it to the reader's imagination. One of the young braves was at once sent off to find the agent, and fetch him to the spot with his cage on wheels. The feat, with much difficulty, was accomplished. Bruin was forcibly and very unwillingly thrust into the prison. The balance of the stipulated sum was honourably paid on the spot, and now that bear is—or, if it is not, ought to be—in the Zoological Gardens of New York, London, or Paris, with a printed account of his catching, and a portrait of Little Tim attached to the front of his cage!

CHAPTER X.

SNAKES IN THE GRASS.

IT was a sad but interesting council that was held in the little fortress of "Tim's Folly" the day following that on which the grizzly bear was captured.

The wounded missionary, lying in Big Tim's bed, presided. Beside him, with an expression of profound sorrow on his fine face, sat Whitewing, the prairie chief. Little Tim and his big son sat at his feet. The other Indians were ranged in a semicircle before him.

In one sense it was a red man's council, but there were none of the Indian formalities connected with it, for the prairie chief and his followers had long ago renounced the superstitions and some of the practices of their kindred.

Softswan was not banished from the council chamber, as if unworthy even to listen to the discussions of the "lords of creation," and no pipe of peace was smoked as a preliminary, but a brief, earnest prayer for guidance was put up by the missionary to the Lord of hosts, and subjects more weighty than are usually broached in the councils of savages were discussed.

The preacher's voice was weak, and his countenance pale, but the wonted look of calm confidence was still there.

"Whitewing," he said, raising himself on one elbow, "I will speak as God gives me power, but I am very feeble, and feel that the discussion of our plans must be conducted chiefly by yourself and your friends."

He paused, and the chief, with the usual dignity of the red man, remained silent, waiting for more. Not so little Tim. That worthy, although gifted with all the powers of courage and endurance which mark the best of the American savages, was also endowed with the white man's tendency to assert his right to wag his tongue.

"Cheer up, sir," he said, in a tone of encouragement; "you mustn't let your spirits go down. A good rest here, an' good grub, wi' Softswan's cookin'—to say nothin' o' her nursin'—will put ye all right before long."

"Thanks, Little Tim," returned the missionary, with a smile; "I do cheer up, or rather, God cheers me. Whether I recover or am called home is in His hands; therefore all shall be well. But," he added, turning to the chief, "God has given us brains, hands, materials, and opportunities to work with, therefore must we labour while we can, as if all depended on ourselves. The plans

K

which I had laid out for myself He has seen fit to change, and it now remains for me to point out what I aimed at so that we may accommodate ourselves to His will. Sure am I that, with or without my aid, His work shall be done, and, for the rest—'though He slay me, yet will I trust in Him."

Again he paused, and the Indians uttered that soft "Ho!" of assent with which they were wont to express approval of what was said.

"When I left the settlements of the white men," continued the preacher, "my object was twofold: I wished to see Whitewing, and Little Tim, and Brighteyes, and all the other dear friends whom I had known long ago, before the snows of life's winter had settled on my head, but my main object was to visit Rushing River, the Blackfoot chief, and carry the blessed Gospel to his people, and thus, while seeking the salvation of their souls, also bring about a reconciliation between them and their hereditary foe, Bounding Bull."

"It's Rushin' River as is the enemy," cried Little Tim, interrupting, for when his feelings were excited he was apt to become regardless of time, place, and persons, and the allusion to his son's wife's father—of whom he was very fond—had roused him. "Boundin' Bull would have bin reconciled long ago if Rushin' River would have listened to reason, for he is a Christian, though I'm bound to say he's somethin' of a queer one, havin' notions of his own which it's not easy for other folk to understand."

"In which respect, daddy," remarked Big Tim, using the English tongue for the moment, and allowing the smallest possible smile to play on his lips, "Bounding Bull is not unlike yourself."

"Hold yer tongue, boy, else I'll give you a woppin'," said the father sternly.

"Dumb, daddy, dumb," replied the son meekly.

It was one of the peculiarities of this father and son that they were fond of expressing their regard for each other by indulging now and then in a little very mild "chaff," and the playful threat to give his son a "woppin'"—which in earlier years he had sometimes done with much effect—was an invariable proof that Little Tim's spirit had been calmed, and his amiability restored.

"My white father's intentions are good," said White-wing, after another pause, "and his faith is strong. It needs strong faith to believe that the man who has shot the preacher shall ever smoke the pipe of peace with Whitewing."

"With God all things are possible," returned the missionary. "And you must not allow enmity to rankle in your own breast, Whitewing, because of me. Besides, it was probably one of Rushing River's braves, and not himself, who shot me. In any case they could not have known who I was."

"I'm not so sure o' that," said Big Tim. "The Blackfoot reptile has a sharp eye, an' father has told me that you knew him once when you was in these parts twenty years ago."

"Yes, I knew him well," returned the preacher, in a low, meditative voice. "He was quite a little boy at the time—not more than ten years of age, I should think, but unusually strong and brave. I met him when travelling alone in the woods, and it so happened that I had the good fortune to save his life by shooting a brown bear which he had wounded, and which was on the point of killing him. I dwelt with him and his people for a time, and pressed him to accept salvation through Jesus, but he refused. The Holy Spirit had not opened his eyes, yet I felt and still feel assured that that time will come. But it has not come yet, if all that I have heard of him be true. You may depend upon it, however, that he did not shoot me knowingly."

Both Little and Big Tim by their looks showed that their belief in Rushing River's future reformation was very weak, though they said nothing, and the Indians maintained such imperturbable gravity that their looks gave no indication as to the state of their minds.

"My white father's hopes and desires are good," said

Whitewing, after another long pause, during which the missionary closed his eyes, and appeared to be resting, and Tim and his son looked gravely at each other, for that rest seemed to them strongly to resemble death. "And now what does my father propose to do?"

"My course is clear," answered the wounded man, opening his eyes with a bright, cheerful look. "I cannot move. Here God has placed me, and here I must remain till—till I get well. All the action must be on your part, Whitewing, and that of your friends. But I shall not be idle or useless as long as life and breath are left to enable me to pray."

There was another decided note of approval from the Indians, for they had already learned the value of prayer.

"The first step I would wish you to take, however," continued the missionary, "is to go and bring to this hut my sweet friend Brighteyes and your own mother, Whitewing, who, you tell me, is still alive."

"The loved old one still lives," returned the Indian.

"Lives!" interposed Little Tim, with emphasis, "I should think she does, an' flourishes too, though she *has* shrivelled up a bit since you saw her last. Why, she's so old now that we 've changed her name to Live-for-ever. She sleeps like a top, an' feeds like a grampus, an' does little else but laugh at what's goin' on around her. I never did see such a jolly old girl in all my life. Twenty years ago—that time, you remember, when Whitewing carried her off on horseback, when the village was attacked —we all thought she was on her last legs, but, bless you sir, she can still stump about the camp in a tremblin' sort o' way, an' her peepers are every bit as black as those of my own Brighteyes, an' they twinkle a deal more."

"Your account of her," returned the preacher, with a little smile, "makes me long to see her again. Indeed, the sight of these two would comfort me greatly whether I live or die. They are not far distant from here, you say ?"

"Not far. My father's wish shall be gratified," said Whitewing. "After they come we will consult again, and my father will be able to decide what course to pursue in winning over the Blackfeet."

Of course the two Tims and all the others were quite willing to follow the lead of the prairie chief, so it was finally arranged that a party should be sent to the camp of the Indians, with whom Brighteyes and Live-for-ever were sojourning at the time—about a long day's march from the little fortress—and bring those women to the hut, that they might once again see and gladden the heart of the man whom they had formerly known as the Preacher.

Now, it is a well-ascertained and undoubtable fact that the passion of love animates the bosoms of red men as well as white. It is also a curious coincidence that this passion frequently leads to modifications of action and un-expected, sometimes complicated, results and situations among the red as well as among the white men.

Bearing this in mind, the reader will be better able to understand why Rushing River, in making a raid upon his enemies, and while creeping serpent-like through the grass in order to reconnoitre previous to a night attack, came to a sudden stop on beholding a young girl playing with a much younger girl—indeed, a little child—on the outskirts of the camp.

It was the old story over again. Love at first sight! And no wonder, for the young girl, though only an Indian, was unusually graceful and pretty, being a daughter of Little Tim and Brighteyes. From the former, Moonlight (as she was named) inherited the free-and-easy yet modest carriage of the pale-face, from the latter a pretty little straight nose and a pair of gorgeous black eyes that seemed to sparkle with a private sunshine of their own.

Rushing River, although a good-looking, stalwart man in the prime of life, had never been smitten in this way before. He therefore resolved at once to make the girl his wife. Red men have a peculiar way of settling such matters sometimes, without much regard to the wishes of the lady—especially if she be, as in this case, the daughter of a foe. In pursuance of his purpose, he planned, while lying there like a snake in the grass, to seize and carry off the fair Moonlight by force, instead of killing and scalping the whole of the Indians in Bounding Bull's camp with whom she sojourned.

It was not any tender consideration for his foes, we are sorry to say, that induced this change of purpose, but the knowledge that in a night attack bullets and arrows are apt to fly indiscriminately on men, women, and children. He would have carried poor Moonlight off then and there if she had not been too near the camp to permit of his doing so without great risk of discovery. The presence of the little child also increased the risk. He might, indeed, have easily "got rid" of her, but there was a soft spot in that red man's heart which forbade the savage deed— a spot which had been created at that time, long, long ago, when the white preacher had discoursed to him of "righteousness and temperance and judgment to come."

Little Skipping Rabbit, as she was called, was the youngest child of Bounding Bull. If Rushing River had known this, he would probably have hardened his heart, and struck at his enemy through the child, but fortunately he did not know it.

Retiring cautiously from the scene, the Blackfoot chief determined to bide his time until he should find a good opportunity to pounce upon Moonlight and carry her off quietly. The opportunity came even sooner than he had anticipated.

That night, while he was still prowling round the camp, Whitewing accompanied by Little Tim and a band of Indians arrived.

Bounding Bull received them with an air of dignified satisfaction. He was a grave, tall Indian, whose manner was not at all suggestive of his name, but warriors in times of peace do not resemble the same men in times of war. Whitewing had been the means of inducing him to accept Christianity, and although he was by no means as " queer " a Christian as Little Tim had described him, he was, at all events, queer enough in the eyes of his enemies and his unbelieving friends to prefer peace or arbitration to war, on the ground that it is written, "If possible, as much as lieth in you, live peaceably with all men."

Of course he saw that the "if possible" justified self-defence, and might in some circumstances even warrant aggressive action. Such, at all events, was the opinion he expressed at the solemn palaver which was held after the arrival of his friends.

" Whitewing," said he, drawing himself up with flashing eyes and extended hand in the course of the debate, "surely you do not tell me that the Book teaches us to allow our enemies to raid in our lands, to carry off our women and little ones, and to burn our wigwams, while we sit still and wait till they are pleased to take our scalps ? "

Having put this rather startling question, he subsided as promptly as he had burst forth.

"That's a poser!" thought the irreverent Little Tim, who sympathised with Bounding Bull, but he said nothing.

"My brother has been well named," replied the uncompromising Whitewing; "he not only bounds upon his foes, but lets his mind bound to foolish conclusions. The Book teaches peace—if possible. If it be not possible, then we cannot avoid war. But how can we know what is possible unless we try? My brother advises that we should go on the war-path at once, and drive the Blackfeet away. Has Bounding Bull tried his best to bring them to reason? Has he failed? Does he know that peace is *impossible?*"

"Now look here, Whitewing," broke in Little Tim at this point. "It's all very well for you to talk' about peace an' what's possible. I'm a Christian man myself, an' there's nobody as would be better pleased than me to see all the redskins in the mountains an' on the prairies at peace wi' one another. But you won't get me to believe that a few soft words are goin' to make Rushin' River all straight. He's the sworn enemy o' Boundin' Bull. Hates him like pison. He hates me like brimstone, an' it's my opinion that if we don't make away wi' him he'll make away wi' us."

Whitewing—who was fond of silencing his opponents by quoting Scripture, many passages of which he had learned by heart long ago from his friend the preacher—did not reply for a few seconds. Then, looking earnestly at his brother chief, he said—

"With Manitou all things are possible. A soft answer turns away wrath."

Bounding Bull pondered the words. Little Tim gave vent to a doubtful "humph"—not that he doubted the truth of the Word, but that he doubted its applicability on the present occasion.

It was finally agreed that the question should not be decided until the whole council had returned to Tim's Folly, and laid the matter before the wounded missionary.

Then Little Tim, being freed from the cares of state, went to solace himself with domesticity.

Moonlight was Indian enough to know that females might not dare to interrupt the solemn council. She was also white woman enough to scorn the humble gait and ways of her red kindred, and to run eagerly to meet her sire as if she had been an out-and-out white girl. The hunter, as we have said, rather prided himself in keeping up some of the ways of his own race. Among other things, he treated his wife and daughter after the manner of white men—that is, well-behaved white men. When Moonlight saw him coming towards his wigwam, she bounded towards him. Little Tim extended his arms, caught her round the slender waist with his big strong hands, and lifted her as if she had been a child until her face was opposite his own.

" Hallo, little beam of light ! " he exclaimed, kissing her on each cheek, and then on the point of her tiny nose.

> "Eyes of mother—heart of sire,
> Fit to set the world on fire."

Tim had become poetical as he grew older, and sometimes tried to throw his flashing thoughts into couplets. He spoke to his daughter in English, and, like Big Tim with his wife, required her to converse with him in that language.

" Is mother at home ? "

" Yes, dear fasser, mosser's at home."

" An' how's your little doll Skippin' Rabbit ? "

" Oh ! she well as could be, an' a'most as wild too as rabbits. Runs away from me, so I kin hardly kitch her sometime."

Moonlight accompanied this remark with a merry laugh, as she thought of some of the eccentricities of her little companion.

Entering the wigwam, Little Tim found Brighteyes engaged with an iron pot, from which arose savoury odours. She had been as lithe and active as Moonlight once, and was still handsome and matronly. The eyes, however,

from which she derived her name, still shone with un-
diminished lustre and benignity.

"Bless you, old woman," said the hunter, giving his
wife a hearty kiss, "you 're as fond o' victuals as ever, I
see."

"At least my husband is, so I keep the pot boiling,"
retorted Brighteyes, with a smile, that proved her teeth to
be as white as in days of yore.

"Right, old girl, right. Your husband is about as good
at emptying the pot as he is at filling it. Come, let 's have
some, while I tell you of a journey that 's in store for
you."

"A long one?" asked the wife.

"No, only a day's journey on horseback. You 're goin'
to meet an old friend."

From this point her husband went on to tell about the
arrival and wounding of the preacher, and how he had
expressed an earnest desire to see her.

While they were thus engaged, the prairie chief was
similarly employed enlightening his own mother.

That kind-hearted bundle of shrivelled-up antiquity was
seated on the floor on the one side of a small fire. Her
son sat on the opposite side, gazing at her through the
smoke, with, for an Indian, an unwonted look of deep
affection.

"The snows of too many winters are on my head to go

on journeys now," she said, in a feeble, quavering voice.
"Is it far that my son wants me to go ?"

"Only one day's ride towards the setting sun, thou dear
old one."

Thus tenderly had Christianity, coupled with a naturally affectionate disposition, taught the prairie chief to
address his mother.

"Well, my son, I will go.   Wherever Whitewing leads
I will follow, for he is led by Manitou.   I would go a
long way to meet that good man the pale-face preacher."

"Then to-morrow at sunrise the old one will be ready,
and her son will come for her."

So saying, the chief rose, and stalked solemnly out of
the wigwam.

CHAPTER XI.

THE SNAKES MAKE A DART AND SECURE THEIR VICTIMS.

WHILE the things described in the last chapter were going on in the Indian camp, Rushing River was prowling around it, alternately engaged in observation and meditation, for he was involved in complicated difficulties.

He had come to that region with a large band of followers for the express purpose of scalping his great enemy Bounding Bull and all his kindred, including any visitors who might chance to be with him at the time. After attacking Tim's Folly, and being driven therefrom by its owner's ingenious fireworks, as already related, the chief had sent away his followers to a distance to hunt, having run short of fresh meat. He retained with himself a dozen of his best warriors, men who could glide with noiseless facility like snakes, or fight with the noisy ferocity of fiends. With these he meant to reconnoitre his enemy's camp, and make arrangements for the final assault when his braves should return with meat—for savages, not less than other men, are dependent very much on full stomachs for fighting capacity.

But now a change had come over the spirit of his dream. He had suddenly fallen in love, and that, too, with one of his enemy's women. His love did not, however, extend to the rest of her kindred. Firm as was his resolve to carry off the girl, not less firm was his determination to scalp her family root and branch.

As we have said, he hesitated to attack the camp for fear that mischief might befall the girl on whom he had set his heart. Besides, he would require all his men to enable him to make the attack successfully, and these would not, he knew, return to him until the following day. The arrival of Whitewing and Little Tim with their party still further perplexed him.

He knew by the council that was immediately called, and the preparations that followed, that news of some importance had been brought by the prairie chief, and that action of some sort was immediately to follow; but of course what it all portended he could not divine, and in his uncertainty he feared that Moonlight—whose name of course he did not at that time know—might be spirited away, and he should never see her again. Really, for a Red Indian, he became quite sentimental on the point, and half resolved to collect his dozen warriors, make a neck-or-nothing rush at Bounding Bull, and carry off his scalp and the girl at the same fell swoop.

Cooler reflection, however, told him that the feat was beyond even *his* powers, for he knew well the courage and strength of his foe, and was besides well acquainted with the person and reputation of the prairie chief and Little Tim, both of whom had foiled his plans on former occasions.

Greatly perplexed, therefore, and undetermined as to his course of procedure, Rushing River bade his followers remain in their retreat in a dark part of a tangled thicket, while he should advance with one man still further in the direction of the camp to reconnoitre.

Having reached an elevated spot as near to the enemy as he dared venture without running the risk of being seen by the sentinels, he flung himself down, and crawled towards a tree, whence he could partially observe what went on below. His companion, a youth named Eagle-nose, silently followed his example. This youth was a fine-looking young savage, out on his first war-path, and burning to distinguish himself. Active as a kitten and modest as a girl, he was also quick-witted, and knew when to follow the example of his chief and when to remain inactive—the latter piece of knowledge a comparatively rare gift to the ambitious!

After a prolonged gaze, with the result of nothing

gained, Rushing River was about to retire from the spot as wise as he went, when his companion uttered the slightest possible hiss. He had heard a sound. Next instant the chief heard it, and smiled grimly. We may remark here in passing that the Blackfoot chief was eccentric in many ways. He prided himself on his contempt for the red man's love for paint and feathers, and invariably went on the war-path unpainted and un-adorned. In civilised life he would certainly have been a Radical. How far his objection to paint was influenced by the possession of a manly, handsome countenance, of course we cannot tell.

To clear up the mystery of the sound which had thrilled on the sharp ear of Eaglenose, we will return to the Indian camp, where, after the council, a sumptuous feast of venison steaks and marrow-bones was spread in Bounding Bull's wigwam.

Moonlight not being one of the party, and having already supped, said to her mother that she was going to find Skipping Rabbit and have a run with her. You see, Moonlight, although full seventeen years of age, was still so much of a child as to delight in a scamper with her little friend, the youngest child of Bounding Bull.

"Be careful, my child," said Brighteyes. "Keep within the sentinels; you know that the great Blackfoot is on the war-path."

"Mother," said Moonlight, with the spirit of her little father stirring in her breast, "I don't fear Rushing River more than I do the sighing of the wind among the pine-tops. Is not my father here, and Whitewing? And does not Bounding Bull guard our wigwams?"

Brighteyes said no more. She was pleased with the thorough confidence her daughter had in her natural protectors, and quietly went on with the moccasin which she was embroidering with the dyed quills of the porcupine for Little Tim.

We have said that Moonlight was rather self-willed. She would not indeed absolutely disobey the express commands of her father or mother, but when she had made no promise, she was apt to take her own way, not perceiving that to neglect or to run counter to a parent's known wishes is disobedience.

As the night was fine and the moon bright, our self-willed heroine, with her skipping playmate, rambled about the camp until they got so far in the outskirts as to come upon one of the sentinels. The dark-skinned warrior gravely told her to go back. Had she been any other Indian girl, she would have meekly obeyed at once; but being Little Tim's daughter, she was prone to assert the independence of her white blood, and, to say truth, the young braves stood somewhat in awe of her.

"The Blackfoot does not make war against women,"

said Moonlight, with a touch of lofty scorn in her tone. "Is the young warrior afraid that Rushing River will kill and eat us?"

"The young warrior fears nothing," answered the sentinel, with a dark frown; "but his chief's orders are that no one is to leave or enter the camp, so Moonlight must go home."

"Moonlight will do as she pleases," returned the girl loftily. At the same time, knowing that the man would certainly do his duty, and prevent her from passing the lines, she turned sharply round, and walked away as if about to return to the camp. On getting out of the sentinel's sight, however, she stopped.

"Now, Skipping Rabbit," she said, "you and I will teach that fellow something of the art of war. Will you follow me?"

"Will the little buffalo follow its mother?" returned the child.

"Come, then," said Moonlight, with a slight laugh; "we will go beyond the lines. Do as I do. You are well able to copy the snake."

The girl spoke truly. Both she and Skipping Rabbit had amused themselves so often in imitating the actions of the Indian braves that they could equal if not beat them, at least in those accomplishments which required activity and litheness of motion. Throwing herself on her hands and knees, Moonlight crept forward until she came again in sight of the sentinel. Skipping Rabbit followed her trail like a little shadow. Keeping as far from the man as possible without coming under the observation of the next sentinel, they sank into the long grass, and slowly wormed their way forward so noiselessly that they were soon past the lines, and able to rise and look about with caution.

The girl had no thought of doing more than getting well out of the camp, and then turning about and walking boldly past the young sentinel, just to show that she had defeated him, but at Skipping Rabbit's suggestion she led the way to a neighbouring knoll just to have one look round before going home.

It was on this very knoll that Rushing River and Eaglenose lay, like snakes in the grass.

As the girls drew near, chatting in low, soft, musical tones, the two men lay as motionless as fallen trees. When they were within several yards of them the young Indian glanced at his chief, and pointed with his conveniently prominent feature to Skipping Rabbit. A slight nod was the reply.

On came the unconscious pair, until they almost trod on the prostrate men. Then, before they could imagine what had occurred, each found herself on the ground with a strong hand over her mouth.

It was done so suddenly and effectually that there was no time to utter even the shortest cry.

Without removing their hands for an instant from their mouths, the Indians gathered the girls in their left arms as if they had been a couple of sacks or bundles, and carried them swiftly into the forest, the chief leading, and Eaglenose stepping carefully in his footsteps. It was not a romantic or loverlike way of carrying off a bride, but Red Indian notions of chivalry may be supposed to differ from those of the pale-faces.

After traversing the woods for several miles they came to the spot where Rushing River had left his men. They were unusually excited by the unexpected capture, and, from their animated gestures and glances during the council of war which was immediately held, it was evident to poor Moonlight that her fate would soon be decided.

She and Skipping Rabbit sat cowering together at the foot of the tree where they had been set down. For one moment Moonlight thought of her own lithe and active frame, her powers of running and endurance, and meditated a sudden dash into the woods, but one glance at the agile young brave who had been set to watch her would have induced her to abandon the idea even if the thought of leaving Skipping Rabbit behind had not weighed with her.

MOONLIGHT CARRIED OFF.—Page 166.

In a few minutes Rushing River left his men and approached the tree at the foot of which the captives were seated.

The moon shone full upon his tall figure, and revealed distinctly every feature of his grave, handsome countenance as he approached.

The white spirit of her father stirred within the maiden. Discarding her fears, she rose to meet him with a proud glance, such as was not often seen among Indian girls. Instead of being addressed, however, in the stern voice of command with which a red warrior is apt to speak to an obstreperous squaw, he spoke in a low, soft, respectful tone, which seemed to harmonise well with the gravity of his countenance, and thrilled to the heart of Moonlight. She was what is familiarly expressed in the words "done for." Once more we have to record a case of love at first sight.

True, the inexperienced girl was not aware of her condition. Indeed, if taxed with it, she would probably have scorned to admit the possibility of her entertaining even mild affection—much less love—for any man of the Blackfoot race. Still, she had an uneasy suspicion that something was wrong, and allowed an undercurrent of feeling to run within her, which, if reduced to language, would have perhaps assumed the form, "Well, but he *is* so gentle, so respectful, so very unlike all the braves I have ever seen ; but I hate him, for all that ! Is he not the enemy of my tribe ?"

Moonlight would not have been a daughter of Little Tim had she given in at once. Indeed, if she had known that the man who spoke to her so pleasantly was the renowned Rushing River—the bitter foe of her father and of Bounding Bull—it is almost certain that the indignant tone and manner which she now assumed would have become genuine. But she did not know this ; she only knew from his dress and appearance that the man before her was a Blackfoot, and the knowledge raised the whole Blackfoot race very much in her estimation.

"Is the fair-faced maiden," said Rushing River, referring to the girl's comparatively light complexion, "willing to share the wigwam of a Blackfoot chief ?"

Moonlight received this very decided and unusually civil proposal of marriage with becoming hauteur, for she was still ruffled by the undignified manner in which she had been carried off.

"Does the fawn mate with the wolf ?" she demanded. "Does the chief suppose that the daughter of Little Tim can willingly enter the lodge of a Blackfoot ?"

A gleam of surprise and satisfaction for a moment lighted up the grave countenance of the chief.

"I knew not," he replied, "that the maiden who has fallen into my hands is a child of the brave little pale-face

whose deeds of courage are known all over the mountains
and prairies."

This complimentary reference to her father went far to
soften the maiden's heart, but her sense of outraged dignity
required that she should be loyal to herself as well as to
her tribe, therefore she sniffed haughtily, but did not reply.

"Who is the little one?" asked the chief, pointing to
Skipping Rabbit, who, in a state of considerable alarm, had
taken refuge behind her friend, and only peeped at her
captor.

Moonlight paused for a few seconds before answering,
uncertain whether it would be wiser to say who she was,
or merely to describe her as a child of the tribe. Deciding
on the former course, in the hope of impressing the Blackfoot with a sense of his danger, she said—

"Skipping Rabbit is the daughter of Bounding Bull."
Then, observing another gleam of surprise and triumph
on the chief's face, she added quickly, "and the Blackfoot knows that Bounding Bull and his tribe are very
strong, very courageous, and very revengeful. If Moonlight and Skipping Rabbit are not sent home at once,
there will be war on the mountains and the plains, for
Whitewing, the great chief of the prairies, is just now in
the camp of Bounding Bull with his men. Little Tim, as
you know, is terrible when his wrath is roused. If war
is carried into the hunting-grounds of the Blackfeet, many

scalps will be drying in our lodges before the snows of winter begin to descend. If evil befalls Skipping Rabbit or Moonlight, before another moon is passed Rushing River himself, the chicken-hearted chief of the Blackfeet, will be in the dust with his fathers, and his scalp will fringe the leggings of Little Tim."

We have given but a feeble translation of this speech, which in the Indian tongue was much more powerful; but we cannot give an adequate idea of the tone and graceful gesticulation of the girl as, with flashing orbs and heightened colour, she delivered it. Yet it seemed to have no effect whatever on the man to whom it was spoken. Without replying to it, he gently, almost courteously, took the maiden's hand, and led her to a spot where his men were stationed.

They were all on horseback, ready for an immediate start. Two horses without riders stood in the midst of the group. Leading Moonlight to one of these, Rushing River lifted her by the waist as if she had been a feather, and placed her thereon. Skipping Rabbit he placed in front of Eaglenose. Then, vaulting on to his own steed, he galloped away through the forest, followed closely by the whole band.

Now it so happened that about the same hour another band of horsemen started from the camp of Bounding Bull.

Under the persuasive eloquence of Little Tim, the chief

had made up his mind to set out for the fortress without waiting for daylight.

"You see," Tim had said, "we can't tell whether the preacher is goin' to live or die, an' it would be a pity to risk lettin' him miss seein' the old woman and my wife if he *is* goin' to die; an' if he isn't goin' under this time, why, there's no harm in hurryin' a bit—wi' the moon, too, shinin' like the bottom of a new tin kettle in the sky."

The chief had no objections to make. There were plenty of men to guard the camp, even when a few were withdrawn for the trip. As Whitewing was also willing, the order to mount and ride was given at once.

The absence of Moonlight and Skipping Rabbit had not at the time been sufficiently prolonged to attract notice. If they had been thought of at all, it is probable they were supposed to be in one or other of the wigwams. As the moon could not be counted on beyond a certain time, haste was necessary, and thus it came to pass that the party set forth without any knowledge of the disappearance of the girls.

The "dear old one" was fain to journey like the rest on horseback, but she was so well accustomed to that mode of locomotion that she suffered much less than might have been expected. Besides, her son had taken care to secure for her the quietest, meekest, and most easy-going horse belonging to the tribe—a creature whose natural spirit had been reduced by hardship and age to absolute quiescence, and whose gait had been trained down to something like a hobby-horse amble.

Seated astride of this animal, in gentleman fashion, the mother of Whitewing swayed gently to and fro like a partially revived mummy of an amiable type, with her devoted son on one side and Little Tim on the other, to guard against accidents.

It chanced that the two parties of horsemen journeyed in nearly opposite directions, so that every hour of the night separated them from each other more and more.

It was not until Whitewing's party had proceeded far on their way to Tim's Folly that suspicion began to be aroused and inquiry to be made in the camp. Then, as the two girls were nowhere to be found, the alarm spread; the warriors sallied out, and the trail of the Blackfeet was discovered. It was not, however, until daylight came to their aid that the Indians became fully aware of their loss, and sent out a strong band in pursuit of their enemies, while a messenger was despatched in hot haste to inform Little Tim and Bounding Bull that Moonlight and Skipping Rabbit had been spirited away.

CHAPTER XII.

THE PURSUIT, FAILURE, DESPAIR.

NEVER dreaming of the thunderbolt that was about to be launched, Whitewing, Little Tim, Bounding Bull, and the rest of the party arrived at the little fortress in the gorge.

They found Big Tim on the *qui vive*, and Brighteyes with Whitewing's mother was soon introduced to the wounded preacher.

The meeting of the three was impressive, for not only had they been much attached at the time of the preacher's former visit, but the women were deeply affected by the sad circumstances in which they found their old friend.

"Not much changed, I see, Brighteyes," he said, as the two women sat down on the floor beside his couch. "Only a little stouter; just what might have been expected. God has been kind to you—but, indeed, God is kind to all, only some do not see or believe in the kindness. It is equally kindness in Him whether He sends joy or sorrow, adversity or prosperity. If we only saw the end from the beginning, none of us would quarrel with the way. Love has induced Him to lay me low at present. You have another child, I am told, besides Big Tim?"

"Yes, a daughter—Moonlight we call her," said Bright-eyes, with a pleased look.

"Is she here with you?"

"No; we left her in the camp."

"And my good old friend," he said, turning on his couch, and grasping the withered hand of Whitewing's mother, "how has she prospered in all these years?"

The "old one," who was, as we have said, as deaf as a post, wrinkled her visage up into the most indescribable expression of world-embracing benignity, expanded her old lips, displayed her toothless gums, and chuckled.

"The dear old one," said her son, "bears the snows of many winters on her head. Her brain could not now be touched by the thunders of Niagara. But the eyes are still bright inlets to her soul."

"Bright indeed!" exclaimed the preacher, as he gazed with deep interest at the old face; "wonderful, considering her great age. I trust that these portals may remain unclosed to her latest day on earth."

He was still talking to Whitewing about her when a peculiar whistle was heard outside, as of some water-bird.

Instantly dead silence fell upon all present, and from the fixed gaze and motionless attitude of each it was evident that they anxiously expected a repetition of the sound. It was not repeated, but a moment later voices were heard outside, then a hurried step, and next instant Big Tim sprang into the room.

"A messenger from the camp!" he cried. "Moonlight and Skipping Rabbit have been carried off by Blackfeet."

It could easily be seen at that moment how Bounding Bull had acquired his name. From a sitting posture he sprang to his feet at one bound, darted through the doorway of the hut, cleared the low parapet like a deer, and went down the zigzag path in a succession of leaps that might have shamed a kangaroo. Little Tim followed suit almost as vigorously, accompanying his action with a leonine roar. Big Tim was close on his heels.

"Guard the fort, my son," gasped Little Tim, as he cut the thong that secured his horse at the bottom of the track; "your mother's life is precious, and Softswan's. If you can quit safely, follow up."

Leaping into the saddle, he was next instant on the track of the Indian chief, who had already disappeared.

Hurrying back to the hut, Big Tim proceeded to make hasty preparation for the defence of the place, so that he might be able to join his father. He found the prairie chief standing with closed eyes beside the couch of the preacher, who with folded hands and feeble voice was praying to God for help.

"Is Whitewing indifferent to the misfortunes of his friends," he said somewhat sharply, "that he stands idly by while the Blackfoot robbers carry off our little ones?"

"My son, be not hasty," returned the chief. "Prayer is quite as needful as action. Besides, I know all the land round here—the direction which this youth tells me the enemy have taken, and a short cut over the hills, which will enable you and me to cross the path your father must take, and join him, so that we have plenty of time to make arrangements and talk before we go on the war-path."

The cool, calm way in which the chief spoke, and especially the decided manner in which he referred to a short cut and going on the war-path, tended to quiet Big Tim.

"But what am I to do?" he said, with a look of perplexity. "There are men enough here, no doubt, to hold the place agin a legion o' Blackfeet, but they have no dependable leader."

"Here is a leader on whom you can depend; I know him well," said Whitewing, pointing to the warrior who had brought the news from the camp. "He is a stranger to you, but has been long in my band, and was left by me in the camp to help to guard it in our absence. With him there, I should have thought the stealing of two girls impossible, but he has explained that mystery by telling me that Moonlight crept out of the camp like a serpent, unknown to all, for they found her trail. With Wolf in command and the preacher to give counsel and pray, the women have no cause for fear."

Somewhat reassured, though he still felt uneasy at the thought of leaving Softswan behind him, Big Tim went about his preparations for the defence of the fortress and the rescue of his sister. Such preparations never take much time in the backwoods. In half an hour Wolf and his braves were ready for any amount of odds, and Big Tim was following the prairie chief through the intricacies of the mountains.

These two made such good use of their time that they were successful in intercepting and joining the war-party, which Bounding Bull, with his friend and ally Little Tim, were leading by forced marches on the trail of the Blackfeet.

Rushing River was well aware, however, that such a party would soon be following him. He therefore had advanced likewise by forced marches, because his object was not so much to meet his enemy as to secure his bride. Only let him place her in the safe keeping of his mother with the main body of his tribe, and he would then return on his steps with pleasure, and give battle to his foe.

In this object he was successful. After several days' march he handed over Moonlight and Skipping Rabbit to the care of an old woman, whose countenance was suggestive of wrinkled leather, and whose expression was not compatible with sweetness. It was evident to the captives that Rushing River owed his manly bearing and his comparatively gentle manners not to his mother but to the father, whose scalp, alas! hung drying in the smoke of a foeman's wigwam.

During the forced march the Blackfoot chief had not once opened his lips to the girl he loved. He simply rode by her side, partly perhaps to prevent any sudden attempt at flight, and certainly to offer assistance when difficulties presented themselves on their pathless journey through the great wilderness. And on all such occasions he offered his aid with such grave and dignified gentleness that poor Moonlight became more and more impressed, though, to do her justice, she fought bravely against her tendency to fall in love with her tribal foe.

On reaching home Rushing River, instead of leading his captive to his own wigwam, conducted her, as we have said, to that of his mother. Then, for the first time since the day of the capture, he addressed her with a look of tenderness, which she had never before received except from Little Tim, and, in a minor degree, from her brother.

"Moonlight," he said, "till my return you will be well cared for here by my mother—the mother of Rushing River."

Having said this, he lifted the leathern door of the lodge and went out instantly.

Moonlight had received a terrible shock. Turning quickly to the old woman, she said—

"Was that Rushing River?"

"That," replied the old woman, with a look of magnificent pride, "is my son, Rushing River,—the brave whose name is known far and wide in the mountains and on the plains; whose enemies tremble and grow pale when they hear of him, and who when they see him become dead—or run away!"

Here, then, was a discovery that was almost too much for the unfortunate captive, for this man was the deadly foe of her father and of her brother's father-in-law, Bounding Bull. He was also the sworn enemy of her tribe, and it now became her stern duty, as a true child of the western wilderness, to hate with all her soul the man whom she loved!

Under the impulse of her powerful feelings she sat down, covered her face with her little hands, and—no, she did not burst into tears! Had she been a civilised beauty perhaps she might have done so, but she struggled for a considerable time with Spartan-like resolution to crush down the true feelings of her heart. Old Umqua was quite pleased with the effect of her information, ascribing it as she did to a wrong cause, and felt disposed to be friendly with the captive in consequence.

"My son has carried you off from the camp of some enemy, I doubt not?" she said, in kindly tones.

Moonlight, who had by that time recovered her composure, replied that he had—from the camp of Bounding Bull, whose little daughter he had captured at the same time, and added that she herself was a daughter of Little Tim.

It was now Umqua's turn to be surprised.

"What is that you tell me?" she exclaimed. "Are you the child of the little pale-face whose name extends from the regions of snow to the lands of the hot sun?"

"I am," replied Moonlight, with a look of pride quite equal to and rather more lovely than that of the old woman.

"Ha!" exclaimed Umqua, "you are a lucky girl. I see by my son's look and manner that he intends to take you for his wife. I suppose he has gone away just now, for I saw he was in haste, to scalp your father, and your brother, and Bounding Bull, and all his tribe. After that

he will come home and take you to his wigwam. Rushing River is very brave and very kind to women. The
men laugh at him behind his back—they dare not laugh
before his face—and say he is too kind to them ; but we
women don't agree with that. We know better, and we
are fondest of the kind men, for we see that they are not
less brave than the others. Yes, you are a lucky girl."

Moonlight was not as deeply impressed with her "luck"
as the old lady expected, and was on the point of bursting
out, after the manner of savages, into a torrent of abuse
of the Blackfoot race in general, and of Rushing River in
particular, when the thought that she was a captive and
at the mercy of the Blackfeet fortunately restrained her.
Instead of answering, she cast her eyes on the ground and
remained stolidly silent, by which conduct she got credit
for undeserved modesty.

"Where is the little one of that serpent Bounding
Bull?" asked Umqua, after a brief silence.

"I know not," replied Moonlight, with a look of anxiety.
"When we arrived here Skipping Rabbit was separated
from me. She journeyed under the care of a youth.
They called him, I think, Eaglenose."

"Is Skipping Rabbit the child's name ?"

"Yes."

"Then Skipping Rabbit will skip more than ever, for
Eaglenose is a funny man when not on the war-path, and

his mother is a good woman. She does not talk behind your back like other women. You have nothing to fear for Skipping Rabbit. Come with me, we will visit the mother of Eaglenose."

As the two moved through the Indian camp, Moonlight noticed that the men were collecting and bridling their horses, cleaning and sharpening their weapons, and making preparations generally for an expedition on a large scale. For a moment a feeling of fear filled her heart as she recalled Umqua's remarks about scalping her kindred; but when she reflected how well able her sturdy little father and big brother and Bounding Bull were to take care of themselves, she smiled internally, and dismissed her fears.

Long before they reached Eaglenose's mother's wigwam, Moonlight was surprised to hear the well-known voice of Skipping Rabbit shouting in unrestrained peals of merry laughter. On entering, the cause thereof was at once apparent, for there sat Eaglenose beside his mother (whose nose, by the way, was similar to his own) amusing the child with a home-made jumping-jack. Having seen a toy of this kind during one of his visits to the settlements of the pale-faces, the Blackfoot youth had made mental notes of it, and on his return home had constructed a jumping-jack, which rendered him more popular in his tribe—especially with the youngsters

"THE ABSURD CREATURE THREW UP ITS LEGS."—PAGE 187.

—than if he had been a powerful medicine-man or a noted warrior.

When Moonlight entered, Skipping Rabbit was standing in front of Eaglenose with clasped hands and glittering eyes, shrieking with delight as the absurd creature of wood threw up its legs and arms, kicked its own head, and all but dislocated its own limbs. Catching sight of her friend, however, she gave vent to another shriek with deeper delight in it, and, bounding towards her, sprang into her arms.

Regarding this open display of affection with some surprise, and rightly ascribing it to the influence of white blood in Bounding Bull's camp, Umqua asked Eaglenose's mother if the men were getting ready to go on the warpath.

"I know not. Perhaps my son knows."

Thus directly referred to, Eaglenose, who was but a young warrior just emancipated from boyhood, and who had yet to win his spurs, rose, and, becoming so grave and owlish that his naturally prominent feature seemed to increase in size, said sententiously—

"It is not for squaws to inquire into the plans of *men*, but as there is no secret in what we are going to do, I may tell you, mother, that women and children have not yet learned to live on grass or air. We go just now to procure fresh meat."

So saying, the stripling pitched the jumping-jack into the lap of Skipping Rabbit, and strode out of the lodge with the pomposity of seven chiefs!

That night, when the captives were lying side by side in Umqua's wigwam, gazing at the stars through the hole which was left in the top for the egress of the smoke, Moonlight said to her little friend—

"Does the skipping one know that it is Rushing River who has caught us and carried us away?"

The skipping one said that she had not known, but, now that she did know, she hated him with all her heart.

"So do I," said Moonlight firmly. But Moonlight was wrong, for she hated the man with only a very small portion of her heart, and loved him with all the rest. It was probably some faint recognition of this fact that induced her to add with the intense energy of one who is resolved to walk in the path of duty—"I hate *all* the Blackfeet!"

"So do I," returned the child, and then pausing, slowly added, "except"—and paused again.

"Well, who does the skipping one except?"

"Eaglenose," replied the skipper promptly. "I can't hate *him*, he is such a very funny brave."

After a prolonged silence Moonlight whispered—

"Does Skipping Rabbit sleep?"

"No."

" Is there not something in the great medicine-book that father speaks so much about which teaches that we should love our enemies ? "

" I don't know," replied the little one. "Bounding Bull never taught that to *me*."

Again there was silence, during which Moonlight hoped in a confused sort of way that the teaching might be true. Before she could come to a conclusion on the perplexing point both she and her little friend were in that mysterious region where the human body usually ceases to be troubled by the human mind.

When Bounding Bull and Little Tim found that the Blackfoot chief had escaped them, they experienced what is often termed among Christians a great trial of faith. They did not indeed express their thoughts in language, but they could not quite prevent their looks from betraying their feelings, while in their thoughts they felt sorely tempted to charge God with indifference to their feelings, and even with something like cruelty, in thus permitting the guilty to triumph and the innocent to suffer. The state of mind is not, indeed, unfamiliar to people who are supposed to enjoy higher culture than the inhabitants of the wilderness. Even Whitewing's spirit was depressed for a time, and he could offer no consolation to the bereaved fathers, or find much comfort to himself; yet in the midst of all the mental darkness by which he was at that time surrounded, two sentences which the pale-face missionary had impressed on him gleamed forth now and then, like two flickering stars in a very black sky. The one was, "Shall not the Judge of all the earth do right?" the other, "He doeth all things well." But he did not at that time try to point out the light to his companions.

Burning with rage, mingled somewhat with despair, the white hunter and the red chief returned home in hot haste, bent on collecting a force of men so strong that they would be enabled to go forth with the absolute certainty of rescuing their children, or of avenging them by sweeping the entire Blackfoot nation, root and branch, off the face of the earth, and adorning the garments of their braves with their scalp-locks for ages to come.

It may be easily believed that they did not waste time on the way. Desperate men cannot rest. To halt for a brief space in order to take food and sleep just sufficient to sustain them was all the relaxation they allowed themselves. This was, of course, simply a process of wearing out their strength, but they were very strong men, long inured to hardships, and did not easily wear out.

One night they sat round the camp fire, very weary, and in silence. The fire was low and exceedingly small.

Indeed, they did not dare to venture on a large one while near the enemy's country, and usually contented themselves with a supper of cold, uncooked pemmican. On this night, however, they were more fatigued than usual—perhaps depression of spirit had much to do with it—so they had kindled a fire and warmed their supper.

"What are the thoughts of Bounding Bull?" said Little Tim, at length breaking silence with something like a groan.

"Despair," replied the chief, with a dark frown; "and," he added, with a touch of hesitation, "revenge."

"Your thoughts are not much different from mine," returned the hunter.

"My brothers are not wise," said Whitewing, after another silence. "All that Manitou does to His children is good. I have hope."

"I wish my brother could give me some of his hope. What does he rest his hope on?" asked Little Tim.

"Long ago," answered the chief, "when Rushing River was a boy, the white preacher spoke to him about his soul and the Saviour. The boy's heart was touched. I saw it; I knew it. The seed has lain long in the ground, but it is sure to grow, for it must have been the Spirit of Manitou that touched him; and will He not finish the work that He begins? That is my hope."

The chief's eyes glittered in the firelight while he

spoke. His two companions listened with grave attention, but said no word in reply. Yet it was evident, as they lay down for a few hours' rest, that the scowl of revenge and the writing of despair had alike in some measure departed from the brow of each.

CHAPTER XIII.

THE POWERFUL INFLUENCE OF BAD WEAPONS AND OF LOVE.

WHILE the bereaved parents were thus hastening by forced marches to their own camp, a band of Blackfeet was riding in another direction in quest of buffalo, for their last supply of fresh meat had been nearly consumed. Along with them they took several women to dry the meat and otherwise prepare it. Among these were poor Moonlight and her friend Skipping Rabbit, also their guardian Umqua.

Ever since their arrival in camp Rushing River had not only refrained from speaking to his captives, but had carefully avoided them. Moonlight was pleased at first, but at last she began to wonder why he was so shy, and, having utterly failed in her efforts to hate him, she naturally began to feel a little hurt by his apparent indifference.

Very different was the conduct of Eaglenose, who also accompanied the hunting expedition. That vivacious

N

youth, breaking through all the customs and peculiarities
of Red Indian etiquette, frequently during the journey
came and talked with Moonlight, and seemed to take
special pleasure in amusing Skipping Rabbit.

" Has the skipping one," he said on one occasion,
"brought with her the little man that jumps ?" by which
expression he referred to the jumping-jack.

" Yes, he is with the pack-horses. Does Eaglenose
want to play with him ?"

Oh, she was a sly and precocious little rabbit, who had
used well her opportunities of association with Little Tim
to pick up the ways and manners of the pale-faces—to the
surprise and occasional amusement of her red relations,
whom she frequently scandalised not a little.   Well did
she know how sensitive a young Indian brave is as to his
dignity, how he scorns to be thought childish, and how he
fancies that he looks like a splendid man when he struts
with superhuman gravity, just as a white boy does when
he puts a cigar between his unfledged lips. She thought
she had given a tremendous stab to the dignity of Eaglenose ; and so she had, yet it happened that the dignity of
Eaglenose escaped, because it was shielded by a buckler
of fun so thick that it could not easily be pierced by
shafts of ridicule.

" Yes ; I want to play with him," answered the youth,
with perfect gravity, but a twinkle of the eyes that did not

escape Skipping Rabbit; "I'm fond of playing with him, because he is your little husband, and I want to make friends with the husband of the skipping one; he is so active, and kicks about his arms and legs so well. Does he ever kick his little squaw? I hope not."

"Oh yes, sometimes," returned the child. "He kicked me last night because I said he was so like Eaglenose."

"The little husband did well. A wooden chief so grand did not like to be compared to a poor young brave who has only begun to go on the war-path, and has taken no scalps yet."

The mention of war-path and scalps had the effect of quieting the poor child's tendency to repartee. She thought of her father and Little Tim, and became suddenly grave.

Perceiving and regretting this, the young Indian hastily changed the subject of conversation.

"The Blackfeet," he said, "have heard much about the great pale-faced chief called Leetil Tim. Does the skipping one know Leetil Tim?"

The skipping one, whose good humour was quite restored at the mere mention of her friend's name, said that she not only knew him, but loved him, and had been taught many things by him.

"I suppose he taught you to speak and act like the pale-faced squaws?" said Eaglenose.

" I suppose he did," returned the child, with a laugh, "and Moonlight helped him. But perhaps it is also because I have white blood in me. My mother was a pale-face."

"That accounts for Skipping Rabbit being so ready to laugh, and so fond of fun," said the youth.

" Was the father of Eaglenose a pale-face?" asked the child.

" No ; why ?"

" Because Eaglenose is as ready to laugh and as fond of fun as Skipping Rabbit. If his father was not a pale-face, he could not, I think, have been very red."

What reply the youth would have made to this we cannot tell, for at that moment scouts came in with the news that buffalo had been seen grazing on the plain below.

Instantly the bustle of preparation for the chase began. The women were ordered to encamp and get ready to receive the meat. Scouts were sent out in various directions, and the hunters advanced at a gallop.

The region through which they were passing at the time was marked by that lovely, undulating, park-like scenery which lies in some parts between the rugged slopes of the mountain range and the level expanse of the great prairies. Its surface was diversified by both kinds of landscape —groups of trees, little knolls, stretches of forest, and occasional cliffs, being mingled with wide stretches of grassy plain, with rivulets here and there to add to the wild beauty of the scene.

After a short ride over the level ground the Black-feet came to a fringe of woodland, on the other side of which they were told by the scouts a herd of buffalo had been seen browsing on a vast sweep of open plain.

Riding cautiously through the wood, they came to the edge of it and dismounted, while Rushing River and Eagle-nose advanced alone and on foot to reconnoitre.

Coming soon to that outer fringe of bushes, beyond which there was no cover, they dropped on hands and knees and went forward in that manner until they reached a spot whence a good view of the buffalo could be obtained. The black eyes of the two Indians glittered, and the red of their bronzed faces deepened with emotion as they gazed. And truly it was a sight well calculated to stir to the very centre men whose chief business of life was the chase, and whose principal duty was to procure food for their women and children, for the whole plain away to the horizon was dotted with groups of those monarchs of the western prairies. They were grazing quietly, as though such things as the rattle of guns, the whiz of arrows, the thunder of horse-hoofs, and the yells of savages had never sounded in their ears.

The chief and the young brave exchanged impressive glances, and retired in serpentine fashion from the scene.

A few minutes later, and the entire band of horsemen —some with bows and a few with guns—stood at the outmost edge of the bushes that fringed the forest land. Beyond this there was no cover to enable them to approach nearer to the game without being seen, so preparation was made for a sudden dash.

The huge rugged creatures on the plain continued to browse peacefully, giving an occasional toss to their enormous manes, raising a head now and then, as if to make sure that all was safe, and then continuing to feed, or giving vent to a soft low of satisfaction. It seemed cruel to disturb so much enjoyment and serenity with the hideous sounds of war. But man's necessities must be met. Until Eden's days return there is no deliverance for the lower animals. Vegetarians may reduce their theories to practice in the cities and among cultivated fields, but vegetarians among the red men of the Far West, or the squat men of the Arctic zone, would either have to violate their principles or die.

As Rushing River had no principles on the subject, and was not prepared for voluntary death, he gave a signal to his men, and in an instant every horse was elongated, with ears flat, nostrils distended, and eyes flashing, while the riders bent low, and mingled their black locks with the flying manes.

For a few seconds no sound was heard save the muffled thunder of the hoofs, at which the nearest buffaloes looked up with startled inquiry in their gaze. Another moment, and the danger was appreciated. The mighty host went off with pig-like clumsiness—tails up and manes tossing. Quickly the pace changed to desperate agility as the pursuing savages, unable to restrain themselves, relieved their feelings with terrific yells.

As group after group of astonished animals became aware of the attack and joined in the mad flight, the thunder on the plains swelled louder and louder, until it became one continuous roar—like the sound of a rushing cataract—a bovine Niagara! At first the buffaloes and the horses seemed well matched, but by degrees the superiority of the latter became obvious, as the savages drew nearer and nearer to the flying mass. Soon a puff or two of smoke, a whistling bullet and a whizzing arrow told that the action had begun. Here and there a black spot struggling on the plain gave stronger evidence. Then the hunters and hunted became mixed up, the shots and whizzing were more frequent, the yells more terrible, and the slaughter tremendous. No fear now that Moonlight, and Skipping Rabbit, and Umqua, and all the rest of them, big and little, would not have plenty of juicy steaks and marrow-bones for many days to come.

But all this was not accomplished without some damage to the hunters. Here and there a horse, having put his foot into a badger-hole, was seen to continue his career for a short space like a wheel or a shot hare, while his rider went ahead independently like a bird, and alighted—any-how! Such accidents, however, seldom resulted in much damage, red skin being probably tougher than white, and savage bones less brittle than civilised. At all events, nothing very serious occurred until the plain was pretty well strewn with wounded animals.

Then it was that Eaglenose, in his wild ambition to be-come the best hunter of the tribe, as well as the best warrior, singled out an old bull, and gave chase to him. This was wanton as well as foolish, for bulls are dangerous and their meat is tough. What cared Eaglenose for that? The spirit of his fathers was awakened in him (a bad spirit doubtless), and his blood was up. Besides, Rushing River was close alongside of him, and several emulous braves were close behind.

Eaglenose carried a bow. Urging his steed to the uttermost, he got close up to the bull. Fury was in the creature's little eyes, and madness in its tail. When a buffalo bull cocks its tail with a little bend in the middle thereof, it is time to "look out for squalls."

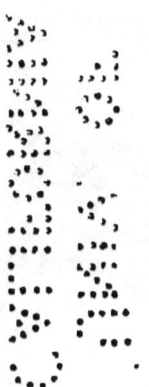

"IT WAS AN AWFUL CRASH."—Page 203.

"Does Eaglenose desire to hunt with his fathers in the happy hunting-grounds?" muttered Rushing River.

"Eaglenose knows not fear," returned the youth boastfully.

As he spoke he bent his bow, and discharged an arrow. He lacked the precision of Robin Hood. The shaft only grazed the bull's shoulder, but that was enough. A Vesuvian explosion seemed to heave in his capacious bosom, and found vent in a furious roar. Round he went like an opera-dancer on one leg, and lowered his shaggy head. The horse's chest went slap against it as might an ocean-billow against a black rock, and the rider, describing a curve with a high trajectory, came heavily down upon his eagle nose.

It was an awful crash, and after it the poor youth lay prone for a few minutes with his injured member in the dust—literally, for he had ploughed completely through the superincumbent turf.

Fortunately for poor Eaglenose, Rushing River carried a gun, with which he shot the bull through the heart and galloped on. So did the other Indians. They were not going to miss the sport for the sake of helping a fallen comrade to rise.

When at last the unfortunate youth raised his head he presented an appearance which would have justified the

change of his name to Turkeycocknose, so severe was the
effect of his fall.

Getting into a sitting posture, the poor fellow at first
looked dazed.　Then observing something between his eyes
that was considerably larger than even he had been accustomed to, he gently raised his hand to his face and
touched it.　The touch was painful, so he desisted.　Then
he arose, remounted his steed, which stood close to him,
looking stupid after the concussion, and followed the
hunt, which by that time was on the horizon.

But something worse was in store for another member
of the band that day.　After killing the buffalo bull, as
before described, the chief Rushing River proceeded to reload his gun.

Now it must be known that in the days we write of the
firearms supplied to the Nor'-west Indians were of very
inferior quality.　They were single flint-lock guns, with
blue-stained barrels of a dangerously brittle character, and
red-painted brass-mounted stocks, that gave them the
appearance of huge toys.　It was a piece of this description
which Rushing River carried, and which he proceeded to
reload in the usual manner—that is, holding the gun under
his left arm, he poured some powder from a horn into his
left palm ; this he poured from his palm into the gun, and,
without wadding or ramming, dropped after the powder a
bullet from his mouth, in which magazine he carried

several bullets so as to be ready. Then driving the butt of the gun violently against the pommel of the saddle, so as to send the whole charge home and cause the weapon to prime itself, he aimed at the buffalo and fired.

Charges thus loosely managed do not always go quite "home." In this case the ball had stuck half-way down, and when the charge exploded the gun burst and carried away the little finger of the chief's left hand. But it did more. A piece of the barrel struck the chief on the head, and he fell from his horse as if he had been shot.

This catastrophe brought the hunt to a speedy close. The Indians assembled round their fallen chief with faces graver, if possible, than usual. They bound up his wounds as well as they could, and made a rough-and-ready stretcher out of two poles and a blanket, in which they carried him into camp. During the greater part of the short journey he was nearly if not quite unconscious. When they at length laid him down in his tent, his mother, although obviously anxious, maintained a stern composure peculiar to her race.

Not so the captive Moonlight. When she saw the apparently dead form of Rushing River carried into his tent, covered with blood and dust, her partially white spirit was not to be restrained. She uttered a sharp cry, which slightly roused the chief, and, springing to his side, went down on her knees and seized his hand. The action was involuntary and almost momentary. She recovered herself at once, and rose quickly, as grave and apparently as unmoved as the reddest of squaws. But Rushing River had noted the fact, and divined the cause. The girl loved him! A new sensation of almost stern joy filled his heart. He turned over on his side without a look or word to any one, and calmly went to sleep.

We have already said, or hinted, that Rushing River was a peculiar savage. He was one of those men—perhaps not so uncommon as we think—who hold the opinion that women are not made to be mere beasts of burden, makers of moccasins and coats, and menders of leggings, cookers of food, and, generally, the slaves of men. One consequence was that he could not bear the subdued looks and almost cringing gait of the Blackfoot belles, and had remained a bachelor up to the date of our story.

He preferred to live with his mother, who, by the way, was also an exception to the ordinary class of squaws. She was rudely intellectual and violently self-assertive, though kind-hearted withal.

That night, when his mother chanced to be alone in the tent, he held some important conversation with her. Moonlight happened to be absent at a jumping-jack entertainment with Skipping Rabbit in the tent of Eagle-nose, the youth himself being the performer in spite of his nose! Most of the other women in the camp were at the place where the buffalo were being cut up and dried and converted into pemmican.

"Mother," said Rushing River, who in reality had been more stunned than injured—excepting, of course, the little finger, which was indeed gone past recovery.

"My son," said Umqua, looking attentively in the chief's eyes.

"The eagle has been brought down at last. Rushing River will be the same man no more. He has been hit in his heart."

"I think not, my son," returned Umqua, looking somewhat anxious. "A piece of the bad gun struck the head of Rushing River, but his breast is sound. Perhaps he is yet stunned, and had better sleep again."

"I want not sleep, mother," replied the chief in figurative language; "it is not the bursting gun that has wounded me, but a spear of light—a moonbeam."

"Moonlight!" exclaimed Umqua, with sudden intelligence.

"Even so, mother; Rushing River has at last found a mate in Moonlight."

"My son is wise," said Umqua.

"I will carry the girl to the camp of mine enemy," continued the chief, "and deliver her to her father."

"My son is a fool," said Umqua.

"Wise, and a fool! Can that be possible, mother?" returned the chief, with a slight smile.

"Yes, quite possible," said the woman promptly. "Man can be wise at one time, foolish at another—wise in one act, foolish in another. To take Moonlight to your tent is wise. I love her. She has brains. She is not like the young Blackfoot squaws, who wag their tongues without ceasing when they have nothing to say and never think—brainless ones!—fools! Their talk is only about each other behind-backs and of feeding."

"The old one is hard upon the young ones," said the chief gravely; "not long ago I heard the name of Umqua issue from a wigwam. The voice that spoke was that of the mother of Eaglenose. Rushing River listens not to squaws' tales, but he cannot stop his ears. The words floated to him with the smoke of their fire. They were, 'Umqua has been very kind to me.' I heard no more."

"The mother of Eaglenose is not such a fool as the rest of them," said Umqua, in a slightly softer tone; "but why does my son talk foolishness about going to the tents of his enemy, and giving up a girl who it is easy to see is good and wise and true, and a hard worker, and *not* a fool?"

"Listen, mother. It is because Moonlight is all that you say, and much more, that I shall send her home. Besides, I have come to know that the pale-face who was shot by one of our braves is the preacher whose words went to my heart when I was a boy. I *must* see him."

"But Bounding Bull and Leetil Tim will certainly kill you."

"Leetil Tim is not like the red men," returned the chief; "he does not love revenge. My enemy Bounding Bull hunts with him much, and has taken some of his spirit. I am a red man. I love revenge because my fathers loved it; but there is something within me that is not satisfied with revenge. I will go alone and unarmed. If they kill me, they shall not be able to say that Rushing River was a coward."

"My son is weak; his fall has injured him."

"Your son is strong, mother. His love for Moonlight has changed him."

"If you go you will surely die, my son."

"I fear not death, mother. I feel that within me which is stronger than death."

CHAPTER XIV.

IN WHICH PLANS, PROSPECTS, LOVE, DANGERS, AND PERPLEXITIES ARE DEALT WITH.

THREE days after the conversation related in the last chapter, a party on horseback, numbering five persons, left the Blackfoot camp, and, entering one of the patches of forest with which the eastern slopes of the mountains were clothed, trotted smartly away in the direction of the rising sun.

The party consisted of Rushing River and his mother, Moonlight, Skipping Rabbit, and Eaglenose.

The latter, although still afflicted with a nose the swelled condition of which rendered it out of all proportion to his face, and interfered somewhat with his vision, was sufficiently recovered to travel, and also to indulge his bantering talk with the "skipping one," as he called his little friend. The chief was likewise restored, excepting the stump of the little finger, which was still bandaged. Umqua had been prevailed on to accompany her son, and it is only just to the poor woman to add that she believed

herself to be riding to a martyr's doom. The chief, however, did not think so, else he would not have asked
her to accompany him.

Each of the party was mounted on a strong horse,
except Skipping Rabbit, who bestrode an active pony
more suited to her size. We say bestrode, because it must
ever be borne in remembrance that Red Indian ladies ride
like gentlemen—very much, no doubt, to their own comfort.

Although Rushing River had resolved to place himself
unarmed in the power of his enemy, he had no intention
of travelling in that helpless condition in a country
where he was liable to meet with foes, not only among
men but among beasts. Besides, as he carried but a
small supply of provisions, he was dependent on gun and
bow for food. Himself, therefore, carried the former
weapon, Eaglenose the latter, and both were fully armed
with hatchet, tomahawk, and scalping-knife.

The path—if such it may be called—which they
followed was one which had been naturally formed by
wild animals and wandering Indians taking the direction
that was least encumbered with obstructions. It was
only wide enough for one to pass at a time, but after the
first belt of woodland had been traversed, it diverged into
a more open country, and finally disappeared, the trees and
shrubs admitting of free passage in all directions.

While in the narrow track the chief had headed the little band. Then came Moonlight, followed by Umqua and by Skipping Rabbit on her pony, Eaglenose bringing up the rear.

On emerging, however, into the open ground, Rushing River drew rein until Moonlight came up alongside of him. Eaglenose, who was quick to profit by example— especially when he liked it—rode up alongside of the skipping one, who welcomed him with a decidedly pale-face smile, which showed that she had two rows of bright little teeth behind her laughing lips.

"Is Moonlight glad," said the chief to the girl, after riding beside her for some time in silence, "is Moonlight glad to return to the camp of Bounding Bull?"

"Yes, I am glad," replied the girl, choosing rather to answer in the matter-of-fact manner of the pale-faces than in the somewhat imaginative style of the Indians. She could adopt either, according to inclination.

There was a long pause, during which no sound was heard save the regular patter of the hoofs on the lawn-like turf as they swept easily out and in among the trees, over the undulations, and down into the hollows, or across the level plains.

"Why is Moonlight glad?" asked the chief.

"Because father and mother are there, and I love them both."

Again there was silence, for Moonlight had replied somewhat brusquely. The truth is that, although rejoicing in the prospect of again seeing her father and mother, the poor girl had a lurking suspicion that a return to them meant final separation from Rushing River, and —although she was too proud to admit, even to herself, that such a thought affected her in any way—she felt very unhappy in the midst of her rejoicing, and knew not what to make of it. This condition of mind, as the reader knows, is apt to make any one lower than an angel somewhat testy!

On coming to a rising ground, up which they had to advance at a walking pace, the chief once more broke silence in a low, soft voice—

"Is not Moonlight sorry to quit the Blackfoot camp?"

The girl was taken by surprise, for she had never before heard an Indian—much less a chief—address a squaw in such a tone, or condescend to such a question. A feeling of self-reproach induced her to reply with some warmth—

"Yes, Rushing River, Moonlight is sorry to quit the lodges of her Blackfoot friends. The snow on the mountain-tops is warmed by the sunshine until it melts and flows down to the flowering plains. The heart of Moonlight was cold and hard when it entered the Blackfoot camp, but the sunshine of kindness has melted it, and now that it flows towards the grassy plains of home, Moonlight thinks with tenderness of the past, and will *never* forget."

Rushing River said no more. Perhaps he thought the reply, coupled with the look and tone, was sufficiently satisfactory. At all events, he continued thereafter to ride in profound silence, and, checking his steed almost imperceptibly, allowed his mother to range up on the other side of him.

Meanwhile Eaglenose and Skipping Rabbit, being influenced by no considerations of delicacy or anything else, kept up a lively conversation in rear. For Eaglenose, like his chief, had freed himself from some of the trammels of savage etiquette.

It would take up too much valuable space to record all the nonsense that these two talked to each other, but a few passages are worthy of notice.

"Skipping one," said the youth, after a brief pause, "what are your thoughts doing?"

"Swelled-nosed one," replied the child, with a laugh at her own inventive genius, "I was thinking what a big hole you must have made in the ground when you got that fall."

"It was not shallow," returned the youth, with assumed gravity. "It was big enough to have buried a rabbit in, even a skipping one."

"Would there have been room for a jumping-jack too?" asked the child, with equal gravity; then, without waiting for an answer, she burst into a merry laugh, and asked where they were travelling to.

"Has not Moonlight told you?"

"No, when I asked her about it yesterday she said she was not quite sure, it would be better not to speak till she knew."

"Moonlight is very wise—almost as wise as a man."

"Yes, wiser even than some men with swelled noses."

It was now the youth's turn to laugh, which he did quite heartily, for an Indian, though with a strong effort to restrain himself.

"We are going, I believe," he said, after a few moments' thought, "to visit your father, Bounding Bull. At least the speech of Rushing River led Eaglenose to think so, but our chief does not say all that is in his mind. He is not a squaw—at least, not a skipping one."

Instead of retorting, the child looked with sudden anxiety into the countenance of her companion.

"Does Rushing River," she asked, with earnest simplicity, "want to have his tongue slit, his eyes poked in, his liver pulled out, and his scalp cut off?"

"I think not," replied Eaglenose, with equal simplicity, for although such a speech from such innocent lips may call forth surprise in a civilised reader, it referred, in those regions and times, to possibilities which were only too probable.

After a few minutes' thought the child said, with an earnest look in her large and lustrous eyes, "Skipping Rabbit will be glad—very glad—to see her father, but she will be sorry—very sorry—to lose her friends."

Having now made it plain that the feelings of both captives had been touched by the kindness of their captors, we will transport them and the reader at once to the neighbourhood of Bounding Bull's camp.

Under the same tree on the outskirts which had been the scene of the girls' capture, Rushing River and Eagle-nose stood once more with their companions, conversing in whispers. The horses had been concealed a long way in rear, to prevent restiveness or an incidental neigh betraying them.

The night was intensely dark and still. The former condition favoured their enterprise, but the latter was unfavourable, as it rendered the risk of detection from any accidental sound much greater.

After a few minutes' talk with his male companion, the chief approached the tree where the females stood silently wondering what their captors meant to do, and earnestly hoping that no evil might befall any one.

"The time has come," he said, "when Moonlight may help to make peace between those who are at war. She knows well how to creep like the serpent in the grass, and how to speak with her tongue in such a way that the heart of the listener will be softened while his ear is charmed. Let Moonlight creep into the camp, and tell Bounding Bull that his enemy is subdued; that the daughter of Leetil Tim has conquered him; that he wishes for friendship, and is ready to visit his wigwam, and smoke the pipe of peace. But tell not that Rushing River is so near. Say only that Moonlight has been set free; that Manitou of the pale-faces has been whispering in the heart of Rushing River, and he no longer delights in revenge or wishes for the scalp of Bounding Bull. Go secretly, for I would not have the warriors know of your return till you have found out the thoughts of the chief. If the ear of the chief is open and his answer is favourable, let Moonlight sound the chirping of a bird, and Rushing River will enter the camp without weapons, and trust himself to the man who was once his foe. If the answer is unfavourable, let her hoot like the owl three times, and Rushing River will go back to the home of his fathers, and see the pleasant face of Moonlight no more."

To say that Moonlight was touched by this speech would give but a feeble description of her feelings. The unusual delicacy of it, for an Indian, the straightforward declaration implied in it, and the pathetic conclusion, would have greatly flattered her self-esteem, even if it had not touched her heart. Yet no sign did she betray of emotion, save the somewhat rapid heaving of her bosom as she stood with bowed head, awaiting further orders.

"Moonlight will find Skipping Rabbit waiting for her here beside this tree. Whether Bounding Bull is for peace or war, Rushing River returns to him his little one. Go, and may the hand of Manitou guide thee."

He turned at once and rejoined Eaglenose, who was standing on guard like a statue at no great distance.

Moonlight went immediately and softly into the bushes, without pausing to utter a single word to her female companions, and disappeared.

Thereupon the chief and his young brave lay down, and, resting there in profound silence, awaited the result with deep but unexpressed anxiety.

Well did our heroine know every bush and rock of the country around her. With easy, soundless motion she glided along like a flitting shadow until she gained the line of sentries who guarded the camp. Here, as on a former occasion, she sank into the grass; and advanced with extreme caution. If she had not possessed more than the average capacity of savages for stalking, it would have been quite impossible for her to have eluded the vigilance of the young warriors. As it was, she narrowly escaped discovery, for, just as she was crossing what may be termed the guarded line, one of the sentinels took it into his head to move in her direction. Of course she stopped and lay perfectly flat and still, but so near did the warrior come in passing that his foot absolutely grazed her head. But for the intense darkness of the night she would have inevitably been caught.

Creeping swiftly out of the sentinel's way before he returned, she gained the centre of the camp, and in a few minutes was close to her father's wigwam. Finding a little hole in the buffalo-skins of which it was chiefly composed, she peeped in.

To her great disappointment, Little Tim was not there, but Brighteyes was, and a youth whom she knew well as one who was about to join the ranks of the men, and go out on his first war-path on the first occasion that offered.

Although trained to observe the gravity and reticence of the Indian, this youth was gifted by nature with powers of loquacity which he found it difficult to suppress. Knowing this, Moonlight felt that she dared not trust him with her secret, and was much perplexed how to attract her mother's attention without disturbing him. At last she crept round to the side of the tent where her mother was seated, opposite to the youth. Putting her lips to another small hole which she found there, she whispered "Mother," so softly that Brighteyes did not hear, but

went calmly on with her needlework, while the aspirant
for Indian honours sent clouds of tobacco from his mouth
and nose, and dreamed of awful deeds of daring, which
were probably destined to end also in smoke.

"Mother!" whispered Moonlight again.

The whisper, though very slightly increased, was
evidently heard, for the woman became suddenly motionless, and turned slightly pale, while her lustrous eyes
gazed at the spot whence the sound had come.

"What does Brighteyes see?" asked the Indian youth,
expelling a cloud from his lips and also gazing.

"I thought I heard—my Moonlight—whisper."

A look of grave contempt settled on the youth's visage
as he replied—

"When love is strong, the eyes are blind and the ears
too open. Brighteyes hears voices in the night air."

Having given utterance to this sage opinion with the
sententious solemnity of an oracle, or the portentous
gravity of "an ass"—as modern slang might put it—the
youth resumed his pipe and continued the stupefaction
of his brain.

The woman was not sorry that her visitor took the
matter thus, for she had felt the imprudence of having
betrayed any symptom of surprise, whatever the sound
might be. When, therefore, another whisper of "Mother!"
was heard, instead of looking intelligent, she bestowed

some increased attention on her work, yawned sleepily once or twice, and then said—

"Is there not a council being held to-night ?"

"There is. The warriors are speaking now."

"Does not the young brave aspire to raising his voice in council ?"

"He does," replied the youth, puffing with a look of almost superhuman dignity, "but he may not raise his voice in council till he has been on the war-path."

"I should have thought," returned Brighteyes, with the slightest possible raising of her eyebrows, "that a brave who aims so high would find it more pleasant to be near the council tent talking with the other young braves than to sit smoking beside a squaw."

The youth took the hint rather indignantly, rose, and strode out of the tent in majestic silence.

No sooner was he gone than Moonlight darted in and fell into her mother's arms. There was certainly more of the pale-face than of the red man's spirit in the embrace that followed; but the spirit of the red man soon reasserted itself.

"Mother," she said eagerly and impressively; "Rushing River is going to be my husband !"

"Child," exclaimed the matron, while her countenance fell, "can the dove mate with the raven ? the rabbit with the wolf ?"

"They can, for all I care or know to the contrary," said
Moonlight—impelled, no doubt, by the spirit of Little
Tim.   "But," she continued quickly, "I bear a message
to Bounding Bull.   Where is he?"

"Not in the camp, my daughter.   He has gone to the
block-house to see the preacher."

"And father.   Is he here?"

"No, he has gone with Bounding Bull.   There is no
chief in the camp just now—only the young braves to
guard it."

"How well they guard it—when I am here!" said the
girl, with a laugh; then, becoming intensely earnest, she
told her mother in as few words as possible the object of
her visit, concluding with the very pertinent question,
"Now, what is to be done?"

"You dare not allow Rushing River to enter the camp
just now," said Brighteyes.   "The young men would
certainly kill him."

"But I must not send him away," returned the perplexed Moonlight.   "If I do, I—I shall never—he will
never more return."

"Could you not creep out of camp as you crept in and
warn him?"

"I could, as far as the sentinels are concerned, for they
are little better than owls; but it is growing lighter now,
and the moon will be up soon—I dare not risk it.   If I

were caught, would not the braves suspect something, and scour the country round? I know not what to do, yet something *must* be done at once."

For some minutes the mother and daughter were silent, each striving to devise some method of escaping from their difficulty. At last Brighteyes spoke.

"I see a way, my child," she said, with more than her wonted solemnity, even when discussing grave matters. "It is full of danger, yet you must take it, for I see that love has taken possession of my Moonlight's heart, and—there is no withstanding love!"

She paused thoughtfully for a few moments, and then resumed—

"One of your father's horses is hobbled down in the willow swamp. He put it there because the feeding is good, and has left no one to guard it because the place is not easily found, as you know, and thieves are not likely to think of it as a likely place. What you must do is to go as near our lines as you dare, and give the signal of the owl. Rushing River will understand it, and go away at once. He will not travel fast, for his heart will be heavy, and revenge to him is no longer sweet. That will give you time to cross the camp, creep past the sentinels, run down to the swamp, mount the horse, and go by the short cuts that you know of until you get in front of the party or overtake them. After that you must lead them to the block-house" (Brighteyes never would consent to call it Tim's Folly after she understood the meaning of the name), "and let the chief manage the rest. Go. You have not a moment to lose."

She gave her daughter a final embrace, pushed her out of the tent, and then sat down with the stoicism of a Red Indian to continue her work and listen intently either for the savage yells which would soon indicate the failure of the enterprise, or the continued silence which would gradually prove its success.

CHAPTER XV.

PLOT AND COUNTERPLOT.

MOONLIGHT sauntered through the camp carelessly at first, with a blanket over her head after the manner of Indian women; but on approaching the outskirts, nearest to the spot where Rushing River was concealed, she discarded the blanket, sank into the grass like a genuine apparition, and disappeared. After creeping a short way, she ventured to give the three hoots of the owl.

An Indian brave, whose eyes were directed sentimentally to the stars, as though he were thinking of his lady-love—or buffalo steaks and marrow-bones—cocked his ears and lowered his gaze to earth, but as nothing more was to be seen or heard, he raised his eyes and thoughts again to love—or marrow-bones.

Very different, as may be supposed, was the effect of those three hoots upon Rushing River, as he lay on the grass in perfect silence, listening intently. On hearing

. P

the sounds, he sprang up as though an arrow had pierced him, and for a few moments the furious glare of a baffled savage gleamed in his dark eyes, as he laid a hand on his tomahawk; but the action was momentary, and in a short time the look passed away. It was succeeded by a calm aspect and demeanour, which seemed to indicate a man devoid of all feeling—good or bad.

"Skipping Rabbit," he said, taking the hand of the child in his, and patting her head, "you are soon to be with your father—and with Moonlight. Rushing River goes back to his people. But the skipping one must not move from this tree till some of her people come to fetch her. There is danger in moving—perfect safety in sitting still."

He moved as if about to go, but suddenly turned back and kissed the child. Then he muttered something in a low tone to his companions, and strode into the dark forest.

Umqua then advanced and gave the little one a tremendous hug. She was evidently struggling to suppress her feelings, for she could hardly speak as she said—

"I—I *must* go, dear child. Rushing River commands. Umqua has no choice but to obey." She could say no more, but, after another prolonged hug, ran rapidly away.

Hitherto Eaglenose had stood motionless, looking on, with his arms folded. Poor boy! he was engaged in the hardest fight that he had yet experienced in his young life, for had he not for the first time found a congenial playmate—if we may venture to put it so—and was she not being torn from him just as he was beginning to understand her value? He had been trained, however, in a school where contempt of pain and suffering was inculcated more sternly even than among the Spartans of old.

"Skipping one," he said, in a low, stern voice, "Eagle-nose must leave you, for his chief commands, but he will laugh and sing no more."

Even through her tears the skipping one could scarce forbear smiling at the tone in which this was uttered. Fortunately, her face could not be seen.

"O yes, you will laugh and sing again," she said, "when your nose is better."

"No, that cannot be," returned the youth, who saw—indeed the child intended—nothing humorous in the remark. "No, I will never more laugh, or pull the string of the jumping-jack; but," he added, with sudden animation, as a thought struck him, "Eaglenose will bring the jumping-jack to the camp of Bounding Bull, and put it in the hands of the skipping one, though his scalp should swing for it in the smoke of her father's wigwam."

He stooped, took the little face between his hands, and kissed it on both cheeks.

"Don't—don't leave me," said the child, beginning to whimper.

"The chief commands, and Eaglenose must obey," said the youth.

He gently unclasped the little hands, and silently glided into the forest.

Meanwhile Moonlight, utterly forgetting amid her anxieties the arrangement about Skipping Rabbit, sauntered back again through the camp till she reached the opposite extremity, which lay nearest to the willow swamp. The lines here were not guarded so carefully, because the nature of the ground rendered that precaution less needful. She therefore managed to pass the sentinels without much difficulty, and found, as she had been told, that one of her father's horses was feeding near the willow swamp. Its two fore-legs were fastened together to prevent it straying, so that she caught it easily. Having provided herself with a strong supple twig, she cut the hobbles, vaulted lightly on the horse's back, and went off at a smart gallop.

Moonlight did not quite agree with her mother as to the effect of disappointment on her lover. Although heaviness of heart might possibly induce him to ride slowly, she thought it much more likely that exasperation of spirit would urge him to ride with reckless fury. Therefore she plied her switch vigorously, and, the light increasing as she came to more open ground, she was able to speed swiftly over a wide stretch of country, with which she had been familiar from childhood, in the hope of intercepting the Blackfoot chief.

After a couple of hours' hard riding, she came to a narrow pass through which she knew her lover must needs go if he wished to return home by the same path that had led him to the camp of his enemy. Jumping quickly from her steed, she went down on her knees and examined the track. A sigh of relief escaped her, for it was evident that no one had passed there that day towards the west. There was just a bare possibility, however, that the chief had taken another route homeward, but Moonlight tried hard to shut her eyes to that fact, and, being sanguine of temperament, she succeeded.

Retiring into a thicket, she tied her horse to a tree, and then returned to watch the track.

While seated there on a fallen tree, thinking with much satisfaction of some of her recent adventures, she suddenly conceived a little plot, which was more consistent with the character of Skipping Rabbit than herself, and rose at once to put it into execution. With a knife which she carried in her girdle she cut and broke down the underwood at the side of the track, and tramped about so as to make a great many footmarks. Then, between that point and the thicket where her steed was concealed, she walked to and fro several times, cutting and breaking the branches as she went, so as to make a wide trail, and suggest the idea of a hand-to-hand conflict having taken place there. She was enabled to make these arrangements all the more easily that the moon was by that time shining brightly, and revealing objects almost as clearly as if it had been noonday.

Returning to the pass, she took off the kerchief with which she usually bound up her luxuriant brown hair, and placed it in the middle of the track, with her knife lying beside it. Having laid this wicked little trap to her satisfaction, she retired to a knoll close at hand, from which she could see her kerchief and knife on the one hand and her horse on the other. Then she concealed herself behind the trunk of a tree.

Now it chanced at that very time that four of the young braves of Bounding Bull's camp, who had been sent out to hunt, were returning home laden with venison, and they happened to cross the trail of Moonlight at a considerable distance from the pass just mentioned. Few things escape the notice of the red men of the west. On seeing the trail, they flung down their loads, examined the prints of the hoofs, rose up, glared at each other, and then ejaculated "Hough!" "Ho!" "Hi!" "Hee!" respectively. After giving vent to these humorous observations, they fixed the fresh meat in the forks of a tree, and, bending forward, followed up the trail like bloodhounds.

Thus it happened that at the very time when Moonlight was preparing her practical joke, or surprise, for Rushing River, these four young braves were looking on with inexpressible astonishment, and preparing something which would indeed be a surprise, but certainly no joke, to herself and to all who might chance to appear upon the scene. With mouths open and eyes stretched to the utmost, these Bounding Bullers—if we may so call them —lay concealed behind a neighbouring mound, and watched the watcher.

Their patience was not put to a severe test. Ere long a distant sound was heard. As it drew near it became distinctly like the pattering sound of galloping steeds. The heart of Moonlight beat high, as she drew closer into the shelter of the tree and clasped her hands. So did the hearts of the Bounding Bullers, as they drew closer under the brow of the mound, and fitted arrows to their bows.

Moonlight was right in her estimate of the effect of disappointment on her lover. He was evidently letting off superfluous steam through the safety-valve of a furious pace. Presently the cavalcade came sweeping into the pass, and went crashing through it—Rushing River, of course, in advance.

No cannon ball was ever stopped more effectually by

mountain or precipice than was our Indian chief's career
by Moonlight's kerchief and knife.   He reined in with
such force as to throw his steed on its haunches, like the
equestrian statue of Peter the Great; but, unlike the
statuesque animal, Rushing River's horse came back to
the position of all-fours, and stood transfixed and trembling.
Vaulting off, the chief ran to the kerchief, and picked it
up.   Then he and Eaglenose examined it and the knife
carefully, after which they turned to the track through
the bushes.   But here caution became necessary.   There
might be an ambuscade.   With tomahawk in one hand,
and scalping-knife in the other, the chief advanced slowly,
step by step, gazing with quick intensity right and left as
he went.   Eaglenose followed, similarly armed, and even
more intensely watchful.   Umqua brought up the rear,
unarmed, it is true, but with her ten fingers curved and
claw-like, as if in readiness for the visage of any possible
assailant, for the old woman was strong and pugnacious
as well as kindly and intellectual.

All this was what some people call "nuts" to Moonlight.   It was equally so to the Bounding Bullers, who,
although mightily taken by surprise, were fully alive to the
fact that here were two men and two women of their
hated Blackfoot foes completely at their mercy.   They
had only to twang their bowstrings and the death-yells of
the men would instantly resound in the forest.   But burn-

ing curiosity as to what it could all mean, and an intense desire to see the play out, restrained them.

Soon Rushing River came upon the tied-up horse, and of course astonishment became intensified, for in all his varied experience of savage warfare he had never seen the evidence of a deadly skirmish terminate in a peacefully-tied-up horse.

While he and his companions were still bending cautiously forward and peering around, the hoot of an owl was heard in the air. Eaglenose looked up with inquiring gaze, but his chief's more practised ear at once understood it. He stood erect, stuck his weapons into his belt, and, with a look of great satisfaction, repeated the cry.

Moonlight responded, and at once ran down to him with a merry laugh. Of course there was a good deal of greeting and gratulation, for even Indians become demonstrative at times, and Moonlight had much of importance to tell.

But now an unforeseen difficulty came in the way of the bloody-minded Bullers. In the group which had been formed by the friendly evolutions of their foes, the women chanced to have placed themselves exactly between them and the men, thus rendering it difficult to shoot the latter without great risk of injury, if not death, to the former, for none of them felt sufficiently expert to emulate William Tell.

In these circumstances it occurred to them, being courageous braves, that four men were more than a match for two, and that therefore it would be safer and equally effective to make a united rush, and brain their enemies as they stood.

No sooner conceived than acted on. Dispensing with the usual yell on this occasion, they drew their knives and tomahawks, and made a tremendous rush. But they had reckoned too confidently, and suffered the inevitable disgrace of bafflement that awaits those who underrate the powers of women. So sudden was the onset that Rushing River had not time to draw and properly use his weapons, but old Umqua, with the speed of light, flung herself on hands and knees in front of the leading Buller, who plunged over her, and drove his head against a tree with such force that he remained there prone and motionless. Thus the chief was so far ready with his tomahawk that a hastily-delivered blow sent the flat of it down on the skull of the succeeding savage, and, in sporting language, dropped him. Thus only two opponents were left, of whom Eaglenose choked one and his chief felled the other.

In ordinary circumstances the victors would first have stabbed and then scalped their foes, but we have pointed out that the spirit of our chief had been changed. He warned Eaglenose not to kill. With his assistance and that of the women, he bound the conquered braves, and laid them in the middle of the track, so that no one could pass that way without seeing them. Then, addressing the one who seemed to be least stunned, he said—

"Rushing River is no longer at war with Bounding Bull. He will not slay and scalp his young men; but the young men have been hasty, and must suffer for it. When your friends find you and set you free, tell them that it was Rushing River who brought Skipping Rabbit to her father and left her near the camp."

"If Rushing River is no longer at war with Bounding Bull," returned the fallen savage sulkily, "how comes it that we have crossed the trail of a war-party of Blackfeet on their way to the block-house of the pale-face?"

This question roused both surprise and concern in the Blackfoot chief, but his features betrayed no emotion of any kind, and the only reply he condescended to make was a recommendation to the youth to remember what he had been told.

When, however, he had left them and got out of hearing, he halted and said—

"Moonlight has travelled in the region of her father's fort since she was a little child. Will she guide me to it by the shortest road she knows?"

The girl of course readily agreed, and, in a few minutes, diverging from the pass, went off in another direction where the ground permitted of their advancing at a swift gallop.

We must turn now to another part of those western wilds, not far from the little hut or fortress named.

In a secluded dell between two spurs of the great mountain range, a council of war was held on the day of which we write by a party of Blackfoot Indians. This particular band had been absent on the war-path for a considerable time, and, having suffered defeat, were returning home rather crestfallen and without scalps. In passing near the fortress of Little Tim it occurred to them that they might yet retrieve their character by assaulting that stronghold and carrying off the booty that was there, with any scalps that chance might throw in their way.

That night the prairie chief, Little and Big Tim, Bounding Bull, and Softswan were sitting in a very disconsolate frame of mind beside their friend the pale-face preacher, whose sunken eye and hollow cheek told of his rapidly approaching end. Besides the prospect of the death of one whom they had known and loved so long, they were almost overwhelmed by despair at the loss of Moonlight and Skipping Rabbit, and their failure to overtake and rescue them, while the difficulty of raising a sufficient number of men at the time to render an attempt upon the Blackfoot stronghold possible with the faintest hope of success still further increased their despair.

Even the dying missionary was scarcely able to give them hope or encouragement, for by that time his voice was so weak that he could only utter a word or two at long intervals with difficulty.

"The clouds are very dark, my father," said Whitewing.

"Very dark," responded his friend, " but on the other side the sun is shining brightly."

"Sometimes I find it rather hard to believe it," muttered Little Tim.

Bounding Bull did not speak, but the stern look of his brow showed that he shared the feelings of the little hunter. Big Tim was also silent, but he glanced at Softswan, and she, as if in reply to his thoughts, said, "He doeth all things well."

"Ha!" exclaimed the missionary, with a quick glance of pleased surprise at the girl; "you have learned a good lesson, soft one. Treasure it. 'He doeth all things well.' We may think some of them dark, some even wrong, but —'Shall not the Judge of all the earth do right?'"

Silence again ensued, for they were indeed very low, yet they had by no means reached the lowest point of human misery. While they were sitting there the Blackfoot band, under cover of the night, was softly creeping up the zigzag path. Great events often turn on small points. Rome was saved by the cackling of geese, and Tim's Folly was lost by the slumbering of a goose! The goose in question

was a youth, who was so inflated with the miraculous nature
of the deeds which he intended to do that he did not give
his mind sufficiently to those which at that time had to
be done.   He was placed as sentinel at the point of the
little rampart furthest from the hut and nearest the forest.
Instead of standing at his post and gazing steadily at the
latter, he sat down and stared dreamily at the future.   As
might have been expected, the first Blackfoot that raised
his head cautiously above the parapet saw the dreamer,
tapped his cranium, and rendered him unconscious.   Next
moment a swarm of black creatures leaped over the wall,
burst open the door of the hut, and, before the men
assembled there could grasp their weapons, overpowered
them by sheer weight of numbers.   All were immediately bound, except the woman and the dying man.

Thus it happened that when Rushing River arrived he
found the place already in possession of his own men.

"I will go up alone," he said, "to see what they are
doing.   If they have got the fire-water of the pale-faces
they might shoot and kill Moonlight in their mad haste."

"If Rushing River wishes to see his men, unseen by them,
Moonlight can guide him by a secret way that is known
only to her father and her father's friends," said the girl.

The chief paused, as if uncertain for a moment how to
act.   Then he said briefly, "Let Moonlight lead; Rushing
River will follow."

Without saying a word, the girl conducted her companion round by the river's bed, and up by the secret path into the cavern at the rear of the little fortress. Here Eaglenose and Umqua were bidden to remain, while the girl raised the stone which covered the upper opening of the cave, and led the chief to the back of the hut, whence issued the sound of voices, as if raised in anger and mutual recrimination.

Placing his eye to a chink in the back door, the Blackfoot chief witnessed a scene which filled him with concern and surprise.

CHAPTER XVI.

THE LAST.

THE sight witnessed by Rushing River was one which might indeed have stirred the spirit of a mere stranger, much more that of one who was well acquainted with, and more or less interested in, all the actors in the scene.

Seated on the floor in a row, with their backs against the wall of the hut, and bound hand and foot, were his old enemies Bounding Bull, Little Tim and his big son, and Whitewing, the prairie chief. In a corner lay a man with closed eyes, clasped hands, and a face the ashy paleness of which indicated the near approach of death, if not its actual presence. In him he at once recognised the preacher, who, years ago, had directed his youthful mind to Jesus, the Saviour of mankind.

In front of these stood one of the warriors of his own nation, brandishing a tomahawk, and apparently threatening instant destruction to Little Tim, who, to do him

justice, met the scowls and threats of the savage with an
unflinching gaze. There was, however, no touch of pride
or defiance in Tim's look, but in the frowns of Bounding
Bull and Big Tim we feel constrained to say that there
were both pride and defiance. Several Blackfoot Indians
stood beside the prisoners with knives in their hands, ready
at a moment's notice to execute their leader's commands.
Rushing River knew that leader to be one of the fiercest
and most cruel of his tribe. Softswan was seated at the
feet of the missionary, with her face bowed upon her
knees. She was not bound, but a savage stood near
to watch her. Whitewing's old mother sat, or rather
crouched, close to her.

What had already passed Rushing River of course
could only guess. Of what followed his ears and eyes
took note.

"You look very brave just now," said the Blackfoot
leader, "but I will make you change your looks before I
take your scalps to dry in the Blackfoot wigwams."

"You had better take our lives at once," said Big Tim
fiercely, "else we will begin to think that we have had
the mischance to fall into the hands of cowardly squaws."

"Wah!" exclaimed Bounding Bull, with a nod of
assent, as he directed a look of scorn at his adversary.

"Tush, tush, boy," said Little Tim to his son reprov-
ingly, in an undertone. "It ill becomes a man with white

Q

blood in his veins, an' who calls hisself a Christian, to go boastin' like an or'nary savage. I thowt I had thrashed that out of 'ee when ye was a small boy."

"Daddy," remonstrated Big Tim, "is not Softswan sittin' there at his marcy?"

"No, lad, no. We are at the marcy of the Lord, an' His marcies are everlastin'."

A faint smile flickered on the lips of the missionary at that moment, and, opening his eyes, he said solemnly—

"My son, hope thou in God, for thou shalt yet praise Him who is the health of thy countenance and thy God."

The savage leader was for the moment startled by the words, uttered in his own language, by one whom he had thought to be dead, but recovering himself quickly, he said—

"Your trust will be vain, for you are now in my power, and I only spare you long enough to tell you that a Blackfoot brave has just met us, who brings us the good news of what our great Blackfoot chief did when he crept into the camp of Bounding Bull and carried away his little daughter from under his very nose, and also the daughter of Leetil Tim. Wah! Did I not say that I would make you change your looks?"

The savage was so far right that this reference to their great loss was a terrible stab, and produced considerable change of expression on the faces of the captives; but with a great effort Bounding Bull resumed his look of contempt, and said that what was news to the Blackfoot leader was no news to him, and that not many days would pass before his warriors would pay a visit to the Blackfoot nation.

" That may be so," retorted the savage, " but they shall not be led by Bounding Bull, for his last hour has come."

So saying, the Blackfoot raised his tomahawk, and advanced to the chief, who drew himself up, and returned his glare of hate with a smile of contempt. Softswan sprang up with a shriek, and would have flung herself between them, but was held back by the savage who guarded her. At that moment the back door of the hut flew open, and Rushing River stood in the midst of them.

One word from him sent all the savages crestfallen out of the hut. He followed them. Returning alone a few seconds later, he passed the astonished captives, and, kneeling down by the couch of the missionary, said, in tones that were too low to be heard by the others—

" Does my white father remember Rushing River ? "

The missionary opened his eyes with a puzzled look of inquiry, and gazed at the Indian's face.

" Rushing River was but a boy," continued the chief, " when the pale-face preacher came to the camp of the Blackfeet."

A gleam of intelligence seemed to shoot from the eyes of the dying man.

"Yes, yes," he said faintly; "I remember."

"My father," continued the chief, "spoke to Rushing River about his sins—about the Great Manitou; about Jesus, the Saviour of all men, and about the Great Spirit. Rushing River did not believe then—he could not—but the Great Spirit must have been whispering to him since, for he believes *now*."

A look of quiet joy settled on the preacher's face while the chief spoke.

Rousing himself with an effort, he said, as he turned a glance towards the captives—

"If you truly love Jesus, let these go free."

The chief had to bend down to catch the feebly-spoken words. Rising instantly, he drew his knife, went to Little Tim, and cut the thongs that bound him. Then he cut those of Big Tim and Whitewing, and lastly those of Bounding Bull.

He had scarcely completed the latter act when his old enemy suddenly snatched the knife out of his hand, caught him by the right arm with a vice-like grasp, and pointed the weapon at his heart.

"Bounding Bull," he said fiercely, "knows not the meaning of all this, but he knows that his child is in the Blackfoot camp, and that Rushing River is at his mercy."

THE DYING MISSIONARY.—Page 244.

No effort did Rushing River make to avert the impending blow, but stood perfectly still, and, with a look of simple gravity, said—

"Skipping Rabbit is not in the Blackfoot camp. She is now in the camp of her kindred; and Moonlight," he added, turning a glance on Little Tim, "is safe."

"Your face looks truthful and your tone sounds honest, Rushing River," said Little Tim, "but the Blackfeet are clever at deceiving, and the chief is our bitter foe. What surety have we that he is not telling lies? Rushing River knows well he has only to give a signal and his red reptiles will swarm in on us, all unarmed as we are, and take our scalps."

"My young men are beyond hearing," returned the chief. "I have sent them away. My breast is open to the knife in the hand of Bounding Bull. I am no longer an enemy, but a follower of Jesus, and the preacher has told us that He is the Prince of peace."

At this the prairie chief stepped forward.

"Friends," he said, "my heart is glad this day, for I am sure that you may trust the word of Rushing River. Something of his change of mind I have heard of in the course of my wanderings, but I had not been sure that there was truth in the report till now."

Still Bounding Bull maintained his grasp on his old

foe, and held the knife in readiness, so that if there should be any sudden attempt at rescue, he, at least, should not escape.

The two Tims, Little and Big, although moved by Whitewing's remarks, were clearly not quite convinced. They seemed uncertain how to view the matter, and were still hesitating when Rushing River again spoke.

"The pale-faces," he said, "do not seem to be so trustful as the red men. I have put myself in your power, yet you do not believe me. Why, then, does not Bounding Bull strike his ancient enemy? His great opportunity has come. His squaws are waiting in his wigwam for the scalp of Rushing River."

For the first time in his life Bounding Bull was rendered incapable of action. In all his extensive experience of Indian warfare he had never been placed in such a predicament. If he had been an out-and-out heathen, he would have known what to do, and would have done it at once—he would have gratified revenge. Had Rushing River been an out-and-out heathen, he never would have given him the chance he now possessed of wreaking his vengeance. Then the thought of Skipping Rabbit filled his heart with tender anxiety, and confused his judgment still more. It was very perplexing! But Rushing River brought the perplexity to an end by saying—

"If you wish for further proof that Rushing River tells no lies, Moonlight will give it. Let her come forward."

Little Tim was beginning to think that the Blackfoot chief was, as he expressed it, somewhat "off his head," when Moonlight ran into the room, and seized him with her wonted energy round the neck.

"Yes, father, it all true. I am safe, as you see, and happy."

"An' Skippin' Rabbit?" said Little Tim.

"Is in her own wigwam by this time."

As she spoke in the Indian tongue, Bounding Bull understood her. He at once let go his hold of his old foe. Returning the knife to him, he grasped his right hand after the manner of the pale-faces, and said—

"My brother."

By this time Eaglenose and Umqua had appeared upon the scene, and added their testimony to that of their chief. While they were still engaged in explanation, a low wail from Softswan turned their attention to the corner where the preacher lay.

The prairie chief glided to the side of his old friend, and kneeled by the couch. The others clustered round in solemn silence. They guessed too surely what had drawn forth the girl's wail. The old man lay, with his thin white locks scattered on the pillow, his hands clasped as if in prayer, and with eyes nearly closed, but the lips moved not.   His days of prayer and striving on this earth were over, and his eternity of praise and glory had begun.

.   .   .   .   .   .

We might here, appropriately enough, close our record of the prairie chief and the preacher, but we feel loath to leave them without a few parting words, for the good work which the preacher had begun was carried on, not only by Whitewing, but, as far as example went—and that was a long way—by Little and Big Tim and their respective wives, and Bounding Bull, as well as by many of their kindred.

After the preacher's remains had been laid in the grave at the foot of a pine-tree in that far western wilderness, Little Tim, with his son and Indian friends, followed Bounding Bull to his camp, where one of the very first persons they saw was Skipping Rabbit, engaged in violently agitating the limbs of her jumping-jack, to the ineffable delight of Eaglenose.

Soon after, diplomatic negotiations were entered into between the tribe of Bounding Bull and the Blackfeet, resulting in a treaty of peace which bid fair to be a lasting treaty, at least as lasting as most other human treaties ever are.   The pipe of peace was solemnly smoked, the war-hatchet was not less solemnly buried, and a feast, on a gigantic scale, was much more solemnly held.

Another result was that Rushing River and Moonlight were married—not after the simple Indian fashion, but with the assistance of a real pale-faced missionary, who was brought from a distance of nearly three hundred miles, from a pale-face pioneer settlement, for the express purpose of tying that knot, along with several other knots of the same kind, and doing what in him lay to establish and strengthen the good work which the old preacher had begun.

Years passed away, and a fur-trading establishment was sent into those western regions, which gradually attracted round it a group of Indians, who not only bartered skins with the traders, but kept them constantly supplied with meat. Among the most active hunters of this group were our friends Little and Big Tim, Bounding Bull, Rushing River, and Eaglenose. Sometimes these hunted singly, sometimes in couples, not unfrequently all together, for they were a very sociable band.

Whitewing was not one of them, for he devoted himself exclusively to wandering about the mountains and prairies, telling men and women and children of the Saviour of sinners, of righteousness and judgment to come—a self-appointed Red Indian missionary, deriving his authority from the Word of God.

But the prairie chief did not forsake his old and well-tried friends. He left a hostage in the little community, a sort of living loadstone, which was sure to bring him back again and again, however far his wanderings might extend. This was a wrinkled specimen of female humanity, which seemed to be absolutely incapable of extinction because of the superhuman warmth of its heart and the intrinsic hilarity of its feelings ! Whoever chanced to inquire for Whitewing, whether in summer or in winter, in autumn or in spring, was sure to receive some such answer as the following : "Nobody knows where he is. He wanders here and there and everywhere ; but he 'll not be absent long, for he always turns up, sooner or later, to see his old mother."

Yes, that mummified old mother, that "dear old one," was a sort of planet round which Brighteyes and Softswan and Moonlight and Skipping Rabbit and others, with a host of little Brighteyes and little Softswans, revolved, forming a grand constellation, which the men of the settlement gazed at and followed as the mariners of old followed the Pole star.

The mention of Skipping Rabbit reminds us that we have something more to say about her.

It so happened that the fur trader who had been sent to establish a post in that region was a good man, and, strange to say, entertained a strong belief that the soul of man was of far greater importance than his body. On the strength of this opinion he gathered the Indians of the neighbourhood around him, and told them that, as he wished to read to them out of the Word of the Great Manitou, he would hold a class twice a week in the fur-store ; and, further, that if any of them wished to learn

English, and read the Bible of the pale-faces for themselves, he was quite willing to teach them.

Well, the very first pupil that came to the English class was Skipping Rabbit, and, curiously enough, the very second was Eaglenose !

Now it must be remembered that we have said that "years had passed away." Skipping Rabbit was no longer a spoiled, little laughing child, but a tall, graceful, modest girl, just bursting into womanhood. She was still as fond as ever of the jumping-jack, but she slily worked its galvanic limbs for the benefit of little children, not for her own—O dear no ! Eaglenose had also grown during these years into a stalwart man, and his chin and lower jaws having developed considerably, his nose was relatively much reduced in appearance. About the same time Brighteyes and Softswan, naturally desiring to become more interesting to their husbands, also joined this class, and they were speedily followed by Moonlight and Bounding Bull. Rushing River also looked in, now and then, in a patronising sort of way, but Whitewing resolutely refused to be troubled with anything when in camp save his mother and his mother-tongue.

It will not therefore surprise the reader to be told that Eaglenose and the skipping one, being thus engaged in a common pursuit, were naturally, we may even say unavoidably, thrown a good deal together; and as their philological acquirements extended, they were wont at times to air their English on each other. The lone woods formed a convenient scene for their intercourse.

"Kom vis me," said Eaglenose to Skipping Rabbit one day after school.

"Var you goes?" asked the girl shyly—yet we might almost say twinklingly.

"Don' know. Nowhars. Everywhars. Anywhars."

"Kim 'long, den."

"Skipping one," said Eaglenose—of course in his own tongue, though he continued the sentence in English— "de lunguish of de pale-fass am diffikilt."

"Yes—'most too diffikilt for larn."

"Bot Softswan larn him easy."

"Bot Softswan have one pale-fass hubsind," replied the girl, breaking into one of her old merry laughs at the trouble they both experienced in communicating through such a "lunguish."

"Would the skipping one," said Eaglenose, with a sharp look, "like to have a hubsind?"

The skipping one looked at her companion with a startled air, blushed, cast down her eyes, and said nothing.

"Come, sit down here," said the Indian, suddenly reverting to his native tongue, as he pointed to the trunk of a fallen tree.

The girl suffered herself to be led to the tree, and sat down beside the youth, who retained one of her hands.

"Does not the skipping one know," he said earnestly, "that for many moons she has been as the sun in the sky to Eaglenose? When she was a little one, and played with the jumping-jack, her eyes seemed to Eaglenose like the stars, and her voice sounded like the rippling water after it has reached the flowering prairie. When the skipping one laughed, did not the heart of Eaglenose jump? and when she let drops fall from her stars, was not his heart heavy? Afterwards, when she began to think and talk of the Great Manitou, did not the Indian's ears tingle and his heart burn? It is true," continued the youth, with a touch of pathos in his tone which went straight to the girl's heart, "it is true that Eaglenose dwells far below the skipping one. He creeps like the beetle on the ground. She flies like the wild swan among the clouds. Eaglenose is not worthy of her; but love is a strong horse that scorns to stop at difficulties. Skipping Rabbit and Eaglenose have the same thoughts, the same God, the same hopes and desires. They have one heart—why should they not have one wigwam?"

Reader, we do not ask you to accept the above declaration as a specimen of Indian love-making. You are probably aware that the red men have a very different and much more prosaic manner of doing things than this. But we have already said that Eaglenose was an eccentric youth; moreover, he was a Christian, and we do not feel bound to account for the conduct or sentiments of people who act under the combined influence of Christianity and eccentricity.

When Skipping Rabbit heard the above declaration, she did indeed blush a little. She could not help that, we suppose, but she did not look awkward, or wait for the gentleman to say more, but, quietly putting her arm round his neck, she raised her little head and kissed that part of his manly face which lay immediately underneath his eagle nose !

Of course he was not shabby enough to retain the kiss. He understood it to be a loan, and returned it immediately with interest—but—surely we have said enough for an intelligent reader !

.   .   .   .   .   .

Not many days after that these two were married in the fur-store of the traders. A grand feast and a great dance followed, as a matter of course. It is noteworthy that there was no drink stronger than tea at that merry-making, yet the revellers were wonderfully uproarious and very happy, and it was universally admitted that, exclusive of course of the bride and bridegroom, the happiest couple there were a wrinkled old woman of fabulous age and her amiable son—the Prairie Chief.

THE END.